THE GUNSMITH

#27

CHINATOWN HELL

THE GUNSMITH

#27

CHINATOWN HELL

J.R. ROBERTS

SPEAKING VOLUMES, LLC
NAPLES, FLORIDA
2013

THE GUNSMITH
#27 CHINATOWN HELL

ISBN 978-1-61232-630-6

To
Mr. Stephen Mertz
and
Mr. Mike Newton

Chapter One

Clint Adams had never wanted to be the Gunsmith. It was a title he'd been given when he was still a lawman in Oklahoma. A reporter learned that young Deputy Adams had a reputation for incredible skill with a six-gun. In fact, the stories were inaccurate—but not because they exaggerated his ability.

The journalist saw an opportunity for a major feature story about Clint Adams. Yet there were many famous lightning-fast gunfighters and the newspaperman realized he'd need to make Clint more colorful to capture the imagination and interest of his readers.

Then he discovered Clint's fascination with firearms. The deputy not only handled a gun with uncanny speed and accuracy, he had also acquired a talent for repairing and modifying firearms as well. This hobby gave the journalist the extra item of special interest needed for his story. Thus the legend of the Gunsmith began.

Clint was basically a modest man, uninterested in fame or glory. His unwanted reputation brought him mountains of trouble. Young gunhawks hunted him out, eager to be known as the man who killed the Gunsmith. Clint tried to avoid such confrontations. Sometimes the trigger-happy youngsters would back down. More often than not, the kids would force Clint to draw his fabled forty-five-caliber Colt which he had personally modified to fire double-action.

This resulted in a lot of dead gunhawks and more

tales to add to the Gunsmith's legend.

Clint's reputation had made his job as a lawman more difficult. Many people considered him a kill-crazy threat, a dangerous man protected by a badge. Others expected him to solve all problems with a gun and they were disappointed when he failed to do so.

After eighteen years as a lawman, Clint Adams gave up the profession, disgusted by the attitudes of the people he was supposed to serve. Yet, ironically, there was only one other occupation Clint was qualified for. He became a genuine gunsmith, traveling throughout the West in his wagon, which served as a combination home and gunsmith shop.

Even as a traveling gunsmith, Clint Adams could not escape his reputation. And, although Clint did not enjoy killing, he had developed the drifter's taste for new horizons, new experiences and new adventures.

The Gunsmith was a free man without ties to family and no responsibilities except those he chose himself. He could go where he pleased and basically do as he pleased. It was a life he had become accustomed to and had no intentions of changing.

However, Clint was born and raised in the East and he occasionally felt a need to return to an environment similar to his cultural roots. More than any other city in the West, San Francisco satisfied this desire.

Clint drove his wagon down Market Street and turned onto Kearney, along the Line. Some of the most famous stores in San Francisco were located on those streets. Clothing, jewelry, leather goods, chinaware and other products were available here. Signs declared the services of attorneys, doctors, dentists and watch-makers.

Many of the buildings were four or five stories tall. Traffic was thick with men on horseback, buggies, wagons and hacks. San Francisco always seemed alive with limitless activity. The dull gray sky above made the excitement and variety of the city seem even more colorful.

At last, Clint found a livery stable on Post Street. He paid the hostler double his usual fee to take care of his gunsmith wagon, team horses and Duke. A magnificent black Arabian gelding, Duke was Clint's most prized possession. The horse was not only big, fast and powerful, he had an almost human intelligence as well.

"Sort of like coming home," Clint said to Duke after he led the gelding into the stall. "Isn't it, big fella?"

Duke wheezed and tossed his head from side to side.

"Okay." The Gunsmith sighed. "I guess you're right at that. San Francisco isn't really a home to either of us. Reckon that wagon and about a million miles of trail dust is the closest thing to a home we're ever going to have."

Clint brushed Duke's glossy black coat and continued to talk to the animal. "Still, we've had some good times here in the past, haven't we? Remember when Jim and I won that bundle of cash in a poker game?" He was referring to James "Wild Bill" Hickok who had been the Gunsmith's best friend. Hickok had been killed two years earlier. Clint had taken the man's death very hard, but he'd learned something after the many hours of mourning and drinking he'd indulged in following Wild Bill's death. Hickok had lived by the gun and died by the gun. The same would one day be true for Clint Adams. And that suited the Gunsmith just fine.

"Hell." Clint shrugged. "Of course you don't remember. You weren't inside the casino. The other card players didn't even know who Jim was. He did the best imitation of an eastern dandy you ever saw. Old Wild Bill was quite a man.''

Duke raised and lowered his head as if to confirm the Gunsmith's statement.

"Well, I'm going to try to blend some business with pleasure while we're here," Clint continued. "Lots of folks in San Francisco and that means there are lots of guns. City folks aren't much for fixing firearms themselves, so I figure I can get some pretty good business while I'm here.''

Duke snorted in reply.

"I know what you're thinking," the Gunsmith said. "There are probably a hundred or more gunsmith shops right here in the city so why will anybody come to me instead of them? I bet you think I just came here to chase the girls, gamble and live high on the hog for a week or two. Is that it?''

Duke seemed to cock his head and stare at Clint as if to ask, "Well?"

"Hey," the Gunsmith began, "you can't tell me that it's a waste of time to try to compete with the local shops until we've seen if it can be done or not. Sure, I plan to have a good time while I'm in town. Not enjoying yourself in San Francisco makes as much sense as wearing your best Sunday suit while you're shoveling horseshit.''

Clint scratched Duke's muzzle. "You just relax here and rest up while I go get myself settled into a hotel for the night. I'll be back and see you in the morning.''

Duke snorted sourly.

"Come on," Clint complained. "You don't think I'm going to get into any trouble the first night I'm in town, do you?''

Duke bobbed his head in reply.

Chapter Two

The Gunsmith checked into a hotel on Sutter Street and left his saddlebags, traveling valise and forty-five caliber Springfield carbine in the room. Since he planned to get a couple drinks and possibly find a card game in progress, Clint had taken the precaution of tucking his belly-gun inside his belt under his shirt. A diminutive New Line Colt, the tiny twenty-two-caliber pistol was an ideal hideout gun.

Although Clint wasn't looking for trouble he realized that a man can find it easily enough in some of the saloons and taverns in San Francisco. The city attracts a mixed crowd, including every type of desperado from pickpocket to professional killers with thieves, outlaws and con artists in between.

Clint didn't have to wander too far to find a place that looked ideal for his needs. The Red Bull Saloon on Bush Street was a big tavern with lead glass windows and hand-carved batwings. The sounds of laughing, cheering customers and a loud piano nearly drowned out the voice of a rather timid singer. *Business must be good*, Clint thought as he pushed through the batwings.

The barroom was enormous with at least three dozen tables and four times as many chairs. The floor was laced with sawdust and the bar itself was so large three bartenders were required to work it. Clint guessed there were over a hundred customers in the place.

Most of these appeared to be stevedores, broad-shouldered men with muscular bodies and powerful backs. A few were cowboys and others were probably shopkeepers and visiting businessmen. Several painted-faced whores tried to get men's attention away from the numerous card games in progress. None of the girls seemed to be doing very well. Clint could see why. A prairie dog in a dress would have had more sex appeal than most of the whores at the Red Bull.

In addition to the bartenders and the prostitutes, there were also about a dozen muscle-bound bouncers with clubs and guns thrust into their belts. They made no effort at subtlety, probably believing that the more dangerous they appeared, the less likely anyone would want to start trouble in the bar. Maybe it worked, but Clint didn't think most of the stevedores would be impressed by the bouncers if a brawl started. They were just as big and tough-looking and there were three times as many stevedores as bouncers.

Two Chinese quietly swept the floor. One was a short wiry man and the other was tall for an Oriental with a muscular physique. They tried to avoid bumping into the customers in the crowded barroom, but occasionally this happened anyway since there were so many customers and a good deal of liquor in most of them.

When the Chinese happened to bump into someone, they bowed humbly and apologized. The customers generally expressed their good will by shoving the Orientals and snarling ethnic slurs. Clint saw one of the stevedores backhand the smaller Chinese across the face.

"You stupid chink bastard," the dockworker spat. "Watch where you're going, damn it!"

"So sorry," the little Chinese replied, bowing before the surly man. "Please excuse please."

"Maybe he can't see so good with them slanty eyes," another stevedore said, laughing. "That your problem, Chinaman?"

"His problem is gonna be me bustin' his friggin' head if'n he don't act straight," the first longshoreman growled. "Don't know why Arnie hires these Chinese shits anyway."

"Maybe there's a shortage of niggers and greasers," the second man chuckled.

"That's wishful thinkin' if'n I ever heard it," the first stated with a grin.

Clint clucked his tongue with disgust. He'd seen Chinese abused before and it turned his stomach. Most Chinese the Gunsmith had encountered were honorable and polite. They were intelligent, hard-working people who generally received little for their labor, yet they always seemed to do the best with what they had.

The Gunsmith moved to the bar and waited for one of the men behind the counter to find time to ask him what he wanted. Finally, a fat, red-faced bartender noticed Clint.

"What'll you have, mate?" the man inquired, his voice flavored by a Cockney accent.

"How's the beer?" Clint asked.

"Bloody awful," the bartender replied. "If you was to ask my opinion, guvnor, I'd advise you to try the red ale instead. Bloody good it is."

"Is that how it got red?"

"Oh." The bartender blinked. "I see, it's a joke 'bout the bloody good ale. That's pretty funny, mate. I'll be tellin' that one to me partners, I will."

"Glad you enjoyed it," Clint said dryly. "I'll try the ale."

"You won't regret it, guvnor," the barkeeper assured him as he drew a mug of ale. It looked like a glass of cherry juice with beer foam on top.

"Keep the change," Clint told the bartender as he gave him a dollar.

"Why, thank you, sir." The Cockney smiled.

"Maybe you can give me a little more advice, friend," Clint began. "If I wanted to get into a nice honest card game where there was lots of money being put on the table, which one of these games would come closest to suiting me?"

"I'd reckon that game over yonder, mate." The bartender pointed a plump finger at a table near the west wall.

Four men dressed in suits with cigars jutting from their mouths sat at the table. None of them smiled as they examined their cards. Maybe they didn't like taking risks with the large stacks of ten dollar bills and silver eagles each man had in front of him. Clint could never understand people who fretted when they gambled. The risk is what makes the game worthwhile.

The player with the largest piles of money before him was a stocky, square-faced man with close-cropped brown hair laced with gray at the temples. Behind him stood three well-dressed hulks. The trio looked like bulls that had been trained to wear clothes and stand upright. If they grew horns they could be sold as livestock.

"Now, all the blokes over at that table have more than a few quid to their names, I can tell you that," the Cockney explained. "See the chap with the bodyguards? He's Charles Madrid. Big Bad Charlie, they calls him and he's all three, believe me."

"What'd he do to earn the title?" Clint asked.

"Charlie owns a chain of leather goods shops found all over San Francisco," the barkeeper answered. "So what's so bad about that, you ask? Nothing except for the fact he makes everybody else on the block deliver a tenth of their weekly profit to the leather shops. Each tannery has bully-boys like those three blokes with Charlie. You either pay Bad Charlie his protection money or you get your face broken."

"I've seen this sort of thing before," Clint commented, recalling a previous encounter with a Corsican syndicate in New Orleans. "I suppose some of the police are on Charlie's payroll?"

"I wouldn't know about that, guvnor. Can't say as I'd be all that surprised to learn of it. Charlie's probably got enough money to buy Buckingham Palace. Dirty bleeder is enough to make you not want to make an honest livin', don't you know."

"Well, Charlie will keep on sucking people dry until folks decide to fight him," the Gunsmith remarked. "Anyway, he doesn't sound like the sort of fella I care to play cards with."

"Oh, the card game is clean enough," the bartender assured Clint. "It's honest too. Those ruddy apes with Charlie see to that."

"No thanks," Clint said. "Tell me about another game."

The taller of the two Chinese servants shuffled across the floor to Bad Charlie's table and swept the surrounding floor space. The other Oriental joined him and the pair began to argue in their native tongue. Because their language includes a great deal of voice inflection the Chinese often sound as if they're asking a question, barking commands and making flat statements all in the same sentence. For this reason their argument sounded confused and unreasonable to the men in the saloon who couldn't understand a word of it.

"Hey, shut up!" Bad Charlie snapped. "Can't you slant-eyed monkeys see we've got a game goin' here?"

The Chinese continued to argue. One threw down his broom in disgust. The other folded his hands on his chest and shook his head.

"*Bu-hau!*" he growled. "*Bu-hau!*"

"Shit." Charlie spat out the stump of his cigar. "Petie, shut those chinks up."

"Okay, Mr. Madrid," one of the bodyguards replied with a slow nod of the head. Clint guessed the goon basically used his head just to nod with. He sure didn't appear to put any strain on the gray matter inside it.

Petie lumbered over to the two Chinese and reached his big dirty hands at the pair, probably to grab their jackets and shake them. Suddenly both Chinese shot out one arm each and snared the hulk's wrists.

Before the slow-witted muscle boy knew what happened, the two Chinese kicked him in the shins, the edges of their slipper-clad feet striking hard. The smaller man slashed the side of his hand into Petie's solar plexus. His taller partner rammed a powerful punch to the point of the thug's jaw. Petie staggered backward and the smaller Oriental whipped a back-fist blow to the dazed goon's face.

Petie fell to the floor like a head-shot ox. The wiry Chinese almost casually kicked him behind the ear and rendered the larger man unconscious. The other two bodyguards reached inside their jackets.

"Don't try it, muscle brains!" the taller Oriental snapped as he thrust a forty-four Smith & Wesson at the pair, the barrel cut down to four inches. "You pull any irons and I'll pull this trigger. If you can't figure that out, ask King Charlie to draw you some pictures:"

"What the hell do you think you're doing, you yellow-faced—" Bad Charlie demanded.

"Keep talking, fella," the Chinese replied, his fluent English containing an accent that was more San Francisco than Canton, "and I'll see if I can shove that cigar up your nose."

"I am John Chang and this is Sam Wing," the smaller Oriental declared as he aimed a short-barreled forty-four Colt at Bad Charlie's chest. "We are detectives for a private company that is legally licensed with the city of San Francisco."

"And by that authority," Sam Wing stated, "we are placing you under arrest, Charlie. You and your three playmates and pet gorillas as well."

"Wait a minute!" one of the card players exclaimed. "I didn't do anything—"

"I must correct you, Mr. Morrison," John Chang replied. "Sam and I heard you telling Mr. Madrid about your illegal business ventures. You offered to supply him with some additional 'leg-breakers' so you could get 'a piece of the pie,' yes?"

"Bad Charlie planned to extend his extortion business to the docks and the other neighborhoods," Wing explained. "John and I heard the whole thing. These jokers were doing more gabbing than a ladies' Sunday tea party."

"You can't prove a thing," Charlie sneered.

"We can testify to what we heard," Chang told him. "And we also heard enough to know where to find more evidence. You really were quite careless, Mr. Madrid."

"Now, all of you gents take your guns out and put them on the table," Wing ordered. "Do it real slow unless one of you wants to try to catch bullets with your teeth.''

The Gunsmith watched the hoodlums pile their weapons onto the table under the watchful eyes of Chang and Wing. Clint nodded with approval. He liked the Chinese detectives' cunning and style.

"Now that's a couple of clever fellas," Clint mused.

"I don't know about that, guvnor," the bartender remarked. "I reckon some of these stevedores aren't going to take kindly to having their boss hauled off. Best be ready to duck, don't you know."

Clint immediately swung his gaze to the stevedores. Sure enough, two of them had just pulled guns from under their shirts. They used other customers for cover, creeping up behind the distracted patrons to poke their guns between the bodies of unsuspecting spectators. The stevedores aimed their weapons at Chang and Wing.

"Watch out!" Clint shouted, snatching his forty-five from hip leather.

Fire spat from the modified Colt. The roar of the pistol startled everyone present. A stevedore howled and grabbed his forearm as a gun hopped out of his hand. He fell to his knees, hugging the bullet-shattered arm.

The other stevedore gunman swung his pistol at the Gunsmith. Clint had no choice. He fired the Colt again and drilled a forty-five round into the man's chest, left of center. The stevedore's corpse slid across the floor, propelled by the impact of the 240-grain bullet.

Bad Charlie and his bodyguards figured the shooting had provided them with a distraction. John Chang and Sam Wing had both pivoted to face their assailants only to see the Gunsmith take care of the stevedores. However, the detectives turned their backs to Bad Charlie and his goons long enough for the trio to make their move.

The bodyguards launched themselves at Chang and Wing while Charlie dove for the weapons on the table. John Chang glimpsed the clawed hand of his assailant and quickly spun, catching the man's wrist in his left hand. Moving with the stevedore's momentum, the little Chinese turned, dropped to one knee and pulled the man's arm.

The bodyguard executed an abrupt somersault and crashed to the floor hard. The man may not have been a mental giant, but he certainly wasn't a quitter. He scrambled up from the floor and attacked Chang again.

John Chang sighed and shook his head as the man lunged at him, head down like a charging bull. Chang's leg snapped out and the heel of his foot crashed into the bodyguard's face. The kick straightened the man's back and blood gushed from his mouth and nostrils. Chang pivoted and delivered a fast side-kick to his opponent's chest, which sent the hoodlum hurtling into a nearby table.

Sam Wing's assailant threw a punch at the detective's head. Wing weaved out of the path of the fist and swung the revolver in his fist. The muzzle hit the bodyguard in the stomach. The man began to double up, but Wing's left arm shot out first. His fist caught the goon on the side of the jaw. Then he opened his hand and chopped the hard edge of his palm under the man's heart. He instantly followed up with a front of the elbow smash to the side of the attacker's skull and finally clubbed his forearm under the dazed man's jawbone. The bodyguard fell unconscious to the floor.

Bad Charlie grabbed for one of the revolvers on the table as Clint Adams dashed forward. The criminal's fingers actually touched the grips of a pistol when the Gunsmith slammed a boot into the edge of the table. The kick drove the furniture into Charlie's soft gut.

The hoodlum leader wheezed in pain, his eyes swelling in their sockets. Clint rammed a fast left jab to the man's mouth and then hooked the same fist into the hinge of his jawbone. Bad Charlie dropped to the floor in a senseless heap.

Two more stevedores attacked the Chinese detectives. A knife-wielding moron lunged at Sam Wing. Unimpressed, the detective simply shot the man in the kneecap. The stevedore dropped his knife and grabbed the smashed leg with both hands. Wing shoved a foot into the wounded man, knocking him across the floor.

"You must have gotten your brain from a Sears Roebuck catalog," the detective muttered.

The other stevedore grabbed a chair and raised it overhead as he attacked John Chang. The detective could have easily shot his assailant, but unlike his partner, he chose to step forward and suddenly dropped down to the floor. His right leg lashed out, striking his opponent's ankles to sweep his feet out from under him. Man and furniture crashed to the floor.

Clint spied another stevedore reach for a bottle of whiskey. The man grabbed it by the neck and raised the bottle to throw it. The double-action forty-five roared once more and the bottle exploded. The stevedore cried out as shattered glass fragments tore into his hand and the right side of his face.

"Anybody else?" the Gunsmith inquired, holding his pistol ready.

Nobody else wanted to volunteer.

Chapter Three

"You're Clint Adams?" Sam Wing stared at the Gunsmith in amazement. "Well, I'll be a son of a Siamese bitch. No wonder you're so good with a gun."

"I will prepare some *soochong* tea for our guest," John Chang began.

After delivering Bad Charlie Madrid and his pals to the police, the Gunsmith was invited by the detectives to join them in a modest celebration in honor of the night's success. They took Clint to their office at the outskirts of Chinatown where they all sat in comfortable armchairs and discussed the incident that brought them together.

"Tea for the Gunsmith?" Wing looked at his partner as if he'd just suggested they serve their guest boiled urine. "I'm getting out the whiskey."

"Alcohol will affect your ability to think and it dulls the senses," Chang said stiffly. "One's reflexes do not recover from consumption of alcohol and regain their peak level until three weeks have passed . . ."

"Uh-huh," Wing muttered. "I'm still getting the whiskey. Want a cigar, Clint?"

"Yeah," the Gunsmith answered. "Thank you."

"Smoking is contrary to *wu-shu*," Chang warned.

"You sound like a nun lecturing a whore, John,"

Wing growled. "My *wu-shu* did all right tonight, in case you didn't notice."

"You had to shoot the man with the knife."

"I didn't *have to*," Wing insisted. "It was easier, that's all. You just wanted to show off."

"Is *wu-shu* what you call that method of fighting you fellas used back at the Red Bull?" Clint inquired.

"Chinese martial arts," Wing explained. "Some westerners are beginning to get interested in it to a degree. They call it Chinese pugilism or *kung fu*—which actually means training for a martial art."

"A friend of mine back in New Orleans is an expert in a form of French kick-boxing calling savate." Clint was referring to Marcel Duboir who had helped him fight the Corsican syndicate. "Is this *wu-shu* similar?"

"*Wu-shu* is not just a way of fighting," Chang explained. "It is a way of life. It teaches discipline and self-control. To learn a martial art one must also learn to respect when it is proper to use it. *Wu-shu* is for self-defense. It must never be used as a tool of aggression."

"I understand." The Gunsmith nodded. "I feel the same way about firearms. If a man carries a gun on his hip, he has a responsibility to use it only if he has to. A fella should never draw his gun unless he doesn't have any other choice and he should never take it out of leather unless he means to use it."

"I've heard you described as a level-headed man," Wing remarked as he poured two shots of whiskey. "I always figured you'd have a lot in common with John and me."

"If he *is* level-headed," Chang said dryly, "what could he have in common with you?"

Wing said something in Chinese which Clint assumed was a rude comment. Chang merely smiled in response.

"How'd you two dream up this detective business?" the Gunsmith asked as he sipped his whiskey.

"Well"—Wing sighed—"John and I are half-breeds. He looks more Chinese than I do, but we're both half white and half Oriental. Our parents moved to the United States in the fifties. My father was a missionary in Canton. He'd gotten the calling to go to China to convert the heathens to Christianity. Instead the heathens converted him."

Wing laughed. "Daddy quit the church and married a Chinese peasant girl. When he saw a chance to return to the United States, he took it. The Manchu tyrants who run the government in China are some of the rottenest bunch of bastards you'd ever want to see— through the sights of a rifle. They would have killed my father if they caught him because he was on close personal terms with several Shaolin priests who managed to escape when the Manchus destroyed their temple in Hu Nan province."

"The Shaolin are a Buddhist order," John Chang explained. "They have helped to develop *wu-shu* ever since the Hou Han Dynasty."

"Warrior priests?" Clint raised an eyebrow.

"Indeed." Chang nodded. "The Shaolin helped to defeat the Mongols. They were very fierce and efficient fighters on the battlefield. Pacifism in the face of tyranny is cowardice. One does not defeat evil with meditation and prayers. It requires action."

"John gets pretty philosophical at times since his father was a student of the Shaolin. Chang Ying-Arng also fled to the United States because the Manchus were after his head."

"He rescued a young American girl from a group of rapists," Chang added. "They soon married."

"Anyway, Clint," Wing said, lighting a match for the Gunsmith's cigar, "half-breeds are always pretty unpopular. Chinese-white combinations aren't any better off than their black, Indian or Mexican counterparts. Bigots—Chinese as well as white—hate your guts because you're living proof of someone of their race copulating with somebody of a race they despise. The whites never really accept you and neither do the Chinese."

"Thus Sam and I were left somewhere between the two cultures," Chang stated. "So we found a profession that would allow us to use our various talents. We are both skilled in *wu-shu* and firearms. We speak both English and Cantonese fluently. I also speak Mandarin and Sam speaks passable Spanish. And we have learned to be like the chameleon. We blend with our surroundings."

"And you decided to become detectives." Clint nodded. "Well, I was pretty impressed by what I saw tonight, except . . ." The Gunsmith hesitated.

"Hey, Clint," Wing said, gesturing with his cigar, "John and I can stand to learn more about how to handle our job. You've got a reputation for doing some pretty impressive detective work yourself. We've heard about your work in Willow Falls and Two Queens. We'd welcome your criticism. Right, John?"

"A man who considers himself too wise to listen to others is a fool," Chang replied.

"That means he agrees," Wing told Clint.

"Okay," the Gunsmith began. "You fellas did a fine job disguised as saloon hands in order to get close enough to listen to Madrid's conversation. But you should have waited until the odds were better before springing your announcement.''

"We wanted to be certain there would be a large number of witnesses to confirm that we were indeed close enough to have heard their conversations,'' Chang explained.

"I understand that.'' The Gunsmith nodded. "But you should have had somebody watch your back. If I hadn't been there, those stevedores might have killed you both.''

"Can't argue with that,'' Wing was forced to admit. "Those guys had us like Sitting Bull and Crazy Horse had Custer at Little Big Horn.''

"Next time,'' Clint continued, "work more closely with the police and have them supply back-up.''

"But we had reason to believe there were police officers in league with Madrid,'' Chang stated.

"Then get some other back-up,'' the Gunsmith told him. "Don't leave your back exposed to attack when you don't know how many enemies you'll have to go up against.''

"You're right, Clint,'' Wing admitted. "We were careless.''

"Nothing wrong with making mistakes,'' Clint said. "Providing you live to learn from them.''

"And man's superior ability to learn is what makes him more than an animal,'' Chang added.

"But it is what we do with what we learn that matters,'' the Gunsmith said, getting into the spirit of the thing.

"Shit,'' Wing muttered sourly. "I need another drink.''

Chapter Four

The detectives invited Clint to continue to celebrate with them. Chang planned to prepare *chou fan* and *shing jen ch'ting*—fried rice and chicken with almonds—and Wing said he could get some lovely and very willing young ladies for the evening. Even so, the Gunsmith declined. He wanted to get up early in the morning and check on Duke before he tried to drum up business for his gunsmith trade.

When Clint returned to the hotel on Sutter Street the desk clerk greeted him with a wide grin and a conspiratorial wink.

"Have a pleasant evening, Mr. Adams?" the clerk inquired.

"Eventful," the Gunsmith replied.

"Your friend is waiting for you in your room." The desk clerk smiled. "You realize this sort of thing is contrary to the rules of this hotel. I don't make the rules, of course, nor do I necessarily agree with the social attitudes that cause certain restrictions in the behavior of our guests—"

"I'd like to know what you're talking about," Clint said, "but I'm getting awful sick of the sound of your voice, fella."

"You don't know about the young lady?" The clerk raised his eyebrows. "But I thought, surely—"

"There's a woman in my room and you just let her go up there?" Clint glared at him. "Probably unlocked the door for her with your passkey too."

"I assumed—"

"If that girl is a thief," the Gunsmith said, "this hotel will have to pay for anything and everything she takes out of that room. And there won't be a hotel in the West that will hire you in the future, fella."

"Oh dear, I'm dreadfully sorry. I'll have her evicted immediately."

"No," Clint said. "I'll talk to her. It is possible a friend of mine sent her over as sort of a gift."

"Oh, I certainly hope so, sir." The desk clerk smiled weakly. "Now, the hotel policy about ladies in a gentleman's room—"

"I'm not paying you to keep your mouth shut," Clint growled. "And if you keep it up, I may just decide to bend the barrel of my gun over your empty skull."

Furious, Clint stomped up the stairs to his room on the third floor. If the girl wasn't a thief, she must have been sent by Sam Wing. The Gunsmith wasn't interested in sleeping with whores, even young attractive ones. He had a personal aversion to this which he himself would have found difficult to explain. Far from a prude about matters of sex, the Gunsmith still found the sale of false affections to be simply a perversion of the act of making love.

Clint unlocked the door and opened it. His right hand dropped to his holstered forty-five and he took care not to stand directly in front of the doorway. Maybe some of Big Bad Charlie's friends had arranged a trap with a girl for bait. Besides, the Gunsmith had enemies everywhere. He'd just lectured Chang and

Wing about the hazards of carelessness. He had no intention of losing his own life because he failed to live by his own advice.

However, the only person inside the room was a pretty Chinese girl. She was small and petite, and her long black hair was fashioned into two pigtails that framed her pale oval face. Large doelike eyes with almond-shaped lids gazed hopefully up at the Gunsmith.

Clint kicked the door shut and checked the room to be certain no one was hiding in the closet or under the bed. The girl stood silently and watched him.

"Okay," Clint began when it seemed the girl wouldn't start the conversation, "who are you and what do you want?"

The girl still stared at him.

"Do you understand English?" the Gunsmith asked, wondering what the hell he'd do if she didn't.

"Yes, Mr. Adams," the girl replied cautiously. "You are Mr. Adams, are you not?"

"That's right." He nodded. "And if you're not going to answer my questions, you can get out of here right now."

"I need your help," she declared.

"Who are you?"

"My name is Su Li," the girl replied. "I have come to see you because it is said you are a very good man. Very brave and a fine warrior who fights for oppressed people."

"Hold on a minute," the Gunsmith told her. "I'm not exactly Robin Hood in denim, lady."

"But I have heard that you helped people many times in the past," Su Li insisted. "Mexican *peones*, Nevada miners, towns where there is no law . . ."

"Occasionally I've found myself in the middle of a lot of trouble and I wound up having to go with one side or the other. Since I have to live with myself for the rest of my life, I let my conscience make the decision for me."

"But you hate evil people, do you not?"

"I usually don't go out of my way to pick a fight with them," the Gunsmith said. "Why don't you just tell me what you want and I'll let you know if I can help or not?"

"I was held prisoner in a brothel," she said as she unbuttoned her pajamalike jacket. "I was beaten and forced to surrender to sexual advances by evil men."

"Wait a minute," Clint said nervously. "Why are you taking your clothes off?"

"To show you what they do to me at that awful place."

The girl stripped off her jacket. Clint gazed at Su Li's small, perfectly formed breasts, their beauty marred by three circular welts on the silken flesh.

"Cigarette burns?" Clint frowned.

"Yes," Su Li replied. "And this."

She turned to display her back. Long diagonal scars crisscrossed her skin. Clint winced. He had once been whipped when El Espectro's *bandidos* held him captive at their stronghold in Mexico. He could appreciate the pain a flogging inflicts.

"How long did they have you in that place?" Clint asked.

"A month," Su Li replied. "Perhaps longer. It is difficult to judge time under such circumstances."

"I can believe that," Clint said. "Why did you come to me instead of the police?"

"I do not trust the police," the girl answered.

"They do not care what happens to Chinese. Besides, some of them are working secretly for the Yellow Serpent Society."

"Yellow Serpent?" Clint frowned. "What's that?"

"Very bad people," Su Li replied. "They captured me and forced me to go with them to a warehouse on the harbor where I was starved and beaten."

"Okay," Clint said. "Kidnapping is against the law whether the person abducted is white, black, Mexican or Oriental."

"That may be what the law says, but Chinese are not equal with whites."

"I know your people aren't treated fairly," Clint agreed. "But no court would approve of kidnapping, assault and torture."

"You're going to take me to the police?" she asked fearfully.

"No," he assured her. "At least not yet. I recently made friends with a pair of detectives. They're both Chinese-Americans. If anybody can help us, John and Sam can."

"But what can they do?"

"More than I can," Clint confessed. "Look, Su Li, I've headed back to San Francisco for a visit just about every year, but I don't live in this city. John and Sam know this place a lot better than I do. They know Chinatown. I'm sure they can find a safe place for you and they probably know some police officers we can trust."

"But detectives cost money to hire," the girl said. "I have no money."

"Don't worry," the Gunsmith said. "I'll cover the expenses."

"I cannot accept charity, Mr. Adams."

"Call me Clint," he urged. "And it isn't charity. Call it a loan until you can afford to pay me back. Besides, Sam and John owe me a favor. Don't worry about it."

"When do we see your detective friends?" Su Li asked. "Tonight?"

"Those two are probably off celebrating right now." Clint smiled. "I doubt that we could find them tonight. We'll go see them in the morning."

"Where will I stay tonight?"

"I guess you'll have to stay here." The Gunsmith shrugged. He tried not to stare at her naked breasts.

"I can never repay you for this, Mr. Clint."

"Just Clint," he told her. "You can probably use a good night's sleep in a feather bed. I'll just set a couple blankets on the floor and pretend it's my bedroll."

"I cannot take your bed from you . . ."

"That's my decision to make," Clint told her. "I'm not going to have a pretty lady sleep on the floor while I have a bed. It is a matter of honor. You understand?"

"Of course." She nodded. "But the bed is large enough for both of us."

"Well, I reckon it is."

"Then why can we not sleep together?"

"No reason." The Gunsmith's eyes wandered over the girl's lovely body. His manhood began to strain against the crotch of his trousers.

"I see you would enjoy pillowing, yes?" Su Li asked, gazing at his erection.

"Pillowing?" He raised an eyebrow.

"It is a more gentle term than sex and more accurate than to say we would be making love. Obviously, you do not love me."

"No, but I like you."

"You need only to want me as I want you."

She stripped off her silk trousers. Clint allowed his gaze to travel over her slender, beautiful body. He eagerly stripped off his own clothing as well.

The girl examined Clint with frank interest. The Gunsmith had seen more than forty summers, yet he looked at least ten years younger than his true age. He was tall and slim with long muscles. Scars from his numerous encounters with violence marred his flesh. The most obvious was the jagged scar on his left cheek which only served to add more character to his ruggedly handsome features.

Su Li glided into Clint's arms. Knowing that many Oriental girls are uncomfortable with kissing on the lips, Clint lowered his mouth to her neck and gently kissed her soft flesh, tracing his tongue along the throbbing cord of arteries under her skin.

The girl responded by taking Clint's hard penis in her hand. She gently stroked it, fondling the fleshy shaft as tenderly as one might a small bird. Gradually, they moved to the bed.

The couple soon lay naked on the mattress. Clint's hands ran along Su Li's soft, smooth skin. His touch slowly became bolder, stroking her breasts and inner thighs.

Su Li kissed Clint's neck and throat. Her tongue traced small circles along his flesh. Their mouths met, tongues dancing fiercely inside each other.

Then Su Li guided the Gunsmith's manhood inside her. He felt his cock sink into her warmth. Clint rotated his hips to gradually work himself deeper. Pacing himself with care, he began to thrust slowly.

Su Li gasped with pleasure and wrapped her legs around him to pull him closer as the Gunsmith lunged faster and harder. She groaned as an orgasm sent a wild tremor through her body. Clint moaned. His throbbing penis fired its load deep inside the girl.

"You pillow nicely, Clint," Su Li whispered as she placed her head against the mat of hair on his chest.

Then the window popped open.

A small, scrawny Chinese slipped silently over the sill. He glanced about the dark room. His eyes expanded fearfully when he saw the Gunsmith staring back at him.

Clint abruptly withdrew from Su Li and leaped from the bed. The Chinese intruder cried out in his native tongue. Clint glimpsed the man's ferret face, decorated by a catfish mustache, an instant before he slammed his fist into it.

The Oriental fell to the floor and reached for the butt of a small pistol in his belt. Clint's bare foot stamped on his wrist before the Chinese could draw his weapon. The little man groaned and snaked his free hand toward the Gunsmith's ankle. Clint's foot moved first, the heel tagging the intruder under the jaw hard.

The Chinese lay dazed as Clint reached down and plucked the gun from his belt. It was an old thirty-six-caliber Navy Colt with a sawed-off barrel. The Gunsmith trained the gun on his opponent and slowly backed away. Su Li screamed.

"Don't worry, honey," he told her. "I've got this bastard covered—"

Suddenly, something slashed from the shadows next to Clint and a forceful blow to his forearm chopped the pistol from his grasp. He turned to see a powerful figure topped by a face that could have been carved in marble. Cold, dark eyes glared at Clint from beneath slanted lids. A wide mouth smiled without mirth and small ears jutted from the side of a shaven bullet-head.

The Gunsmith whirled and lashed a left hook into the larger man's face. The big Oriental's head hardly moved from the punch. Clint swung a right cross. His forearm connected painfully with his opponent's limb as the man easily blocked the second punch.

The bald giant's hand sliced through air. Clint barely saw the attacking limb before the hard edge of the man's hand slammed into the side of his neck. The Gunsmith fell to all fours, the room swirling past his eyes as he felt consciousness melt away. Su Li screamed again.

Then a rock hard fist clubbed Clint behind the ear and he fell on his face. He didn't even feel the carpet when he collapsed onto it.

Chapter Five

"Get up, mister," a voice bellowed from the darkness that engulfed the Gunsmith's consciousness.

He wasn't certain if the sound was real or only a dream. As his senses returned, Clint felt a throbbing pain at the back of his skull. Then a sharp pain lanced through his ribs.

"I said get up, damn it!" the voice snapped. "You've got some explaining to do, Adams!"

Clint slowly pulled himself to a kneeling position and shook his head to clear it. Harsh light stabbed at his eyes as he ventured to open them. Memories flooded back to him suddenly. The Gunsmith abruptly leaped to his feet.

"Easy, Adams," a tall, beefy man dressed in a dark blue uniform warned. "You're not tangling with a young chink gal now."

The policeman aimed a Colt revolver at Clint's chest and thumbed back the hammer. The Gunsmith raised his hands. He realized he was still naked, but he made no attempt to cover his genitals—not while a gun was pointed at him.

"Take it easy, Calley," came another voice. "Don't get nasty unless Adams does something to deserve it."

A man dressed in a tweed suit with a derby perched

31

on his dark blond hair stepped forward. A mustache and mutton chop sideburns covered most of his face, but his eyes were baggy and tired. He opened a leather folder and showed Clint a star-shaped badge.

"Police Inspector Kovac," he announced. "You're in a lot ot trouble, Adams. Better put your clothes on. Because you're coming with us."

"What?" Clint began. "Su Li! Where is she?"

"So that's the girl's name, eh?" Kovac mused.

"She's over there in the bed." Calley smiled coldly. "Where you killed her."

Clint stared at the girl's still body. A blanket had been pulled over her head to cover the face. The Gunsmith stiffened with anger and turned to the two policemen.

"I didn't kill that girl," he declared. "She came to me for help . . ."

"I bet she did," Calley sneered. "A chink girl needs help so she goes out of her way to ask a has-been lawman turned gunfighter if he can give her a hand. Bullshit!"

"That story doesn't wash, Adams," Kovac added as he sat on the corner of the bed and struck a match on the frame to light a cigar. The inspector obviously handled a lot of homicide investigations. Such men frequently develop the habit of smoking cigars to mask the stench of death.

"It's the truth," Clint began.

"You're a stranger in town, Adams," Kovac remarked as he puffed on the cigar. He didn't seem disturbed by the corpse lying beside him, another sign of a veteran homicide investigator. "You just arrived late this afternoon. The hotel register confirms that."

"So what?" the Gunsmith demanded.

"So why would a girl expect to get help from a total stranger who just drifted into town?" Kovac tapped the ash from the end of his cigar. "And you don't exactly have a reputation as a choirboy, Adams."

"I don't have one as a murderer either," Clint stated.

"Ain't that how you make your living, Adams?" Officer Calley asked. "A hired gun is a professional killer, plain and simple."

"Nothing is plain and simple except your ability to think, fella," Clint said angrily.

"You son of a bitch," Calley hissed as he raised the pistol to prepare to strike at Clint.

"Knock it off, Calley!" Kovac snapped. "Don't let him provoke you. That's what he wants. Try to claim the police beat a confession out of him."

"I've got nothing to confess to," Clint said.

"Well, the desk clerk downstairs seems to feel differently," Kovac remarked. "He tells us this girl showed up and asked to go up to your room. He figured she was a whore you sent over, so he let her in. Then you showed up, surly, bad-tempered and angry because he let the girl in your room. You even threatened to assault him with your gun. Right?"

"I figured she might be a thief," Clint said. "When I talked to her, she explained she'd escaped from a brothel."

"What brothel?"

"She didn't say."

"You mean you don't want to say because when we check that whorehouse we'll be told you picked up the girl of her own free will," Kovac said, pointing at Clint with the cigar.

"Goddamn it," Clint snapped. "I'm telling you the

truth. She said something about the Yellow Serpent Society.''

"Everybody in San Francisco has heard of the Yellow Serpents.''

"I'm not from San Francisco, remember?'' Clint said dryly as he pulled on his clothes. "Why don't you enlighten me?''

Kovac sighed. "It's one of the Tongs and you know it.''

"I don't even know what a Tong is,'' the Gunsmith replied. "Let me try to explain a few things. I'm not a gunfighter or a hired killer. I came into town in my gunsmith wagon. I'm here on business—as a gunsmith.''

"Don't you mean *the* Gunsmith?'' Calley sneered.

"I never call myself by that idiot title,'' Clint told him. "But even if I was a hired gun—and I'm not— why would I kill this girl?''

"You were in a bad mood and you'd had too much to drink.'' Kovac shrugged. "Happens all the time. Especially with a man who has a history of violence.''

"I'm not drunk,'' Clint insisted. "I had one glass of whiskey with Sam Wing and John Chang. Check with them if you like. They're detectives—''

"I know who they are.'' Kovac rolled his eyes toward the ceiling. "If you're going to give somebody as a character reference, I suggest you find somebody else.''

"Even if you didn't do much drinkin' with those two half-breeds,'' Calley commented as he shoved a whiskey bottle with his foot, "figure you made up for it when you came back here.''

Clint picked up the bottle. Only a small portion of amber liquid sloshed inside the container. He put the bottle down and glared at the policemen.

"This is a frame," he said. "I'm being set up to take the blame for killing Su Li."

"Come on, Adams," Kovac said. "Who set you up? Why did they do it?"

"Two men broke into the room and attacked me," Clint said.

"Why didn't you shoot them?" Kovac asked.

"I didn't have my gun handy," Clint replied.

"Speaking of which," Kovac said, "get his Colt. The gunbelt too. It isn't evidence in the murder case, but it is evidence that Adams is a quick-draw artist."

"Already got it," Calley confirmed.

"These two guys allegedly broke in." Kovac glanced about the room and shrugged. "Don't see any signs of a struggle."

"They were Chinese," Clint said. "One of them must have been a *wu-shu* expert."

"*Wu-shu*?" Kovac smiled. "You never heard of the Tong but you know about *wu-shu*? Okay, after this Chinese overpowered you, he must have stripped off your clothes and the girl's too. . . ."

"We were already naked," Clint confessed.

"But this girl supposedly came to you for protection," Kovac said in mock astonishment. "She offered you a roll in the hay out of gratitude, I suppose."

"Something like that," Clint was forced to admit.

"Adams, this is the biggest crock of shit I ever heard," Calley snorted.

"Let me get this straight," Kovac said. "You go to bed with the girl and then two Chinese break in. There's no struggle, but they overpower you. Then they strangle the girl and leave the whiskey bottle behind after splashing you and the girl with it so it'll look like you two had a sexual encounter that became violent."

"That's what happened," Clint confirmed.

"Sure it did." Kovac shrugged. "And John Wilkes Booth didn't really kill Lincoln either. It was really a look-alike hired by Union profiteers who wanted Booth to take the rap so everybody would figure he was a crazed Johnny Reb acting alone. Ever hear that story, Adams?"

"There's some folks who believe that's what really happened," Calley added. "Maybe you'll be lucky and the jury will be full of folks who'll believe your bullshit tale too."

"You're not going to listen to me, are you?" The Gunsmith sighed.

"We've been listening, Adams," Kovac said. "And we've sat around here putting up with this nonsense long enough. Finish getting dressed. You're under arrest for murder."

Chapter Six

"Well," the Gunsmith said as he reached inside one of his boots, "I can see it's a waste of time trying to reason with you fellas."

He suddenly pulled his Colt New Line from the boot and aimed it at Officer Calley's face, thumbing back the hammer in a single smooth motion. The startled policeman stared back in disbelief.

"You've got a gun aimed at me and I've got one aimed at you," the Gunsmith declared. "You either pull the trigger or drop the gun. Just remember, if you shoot me, I'll kill you before I die."

"You wouldn't—" Calley began.

"What have I got to lose?" Clint asked.

Calley dropped the gun.

Inspector Kovac yanked a revolver from shoulder leather. Clint hurled his boot at the policeman. It struck his hand and jarred the gun out of Kovac's grasp.

"Hands in the air," the Gunsmith told him, pointing the twenty-two New Line at Kovac.

"Don't be a fool, Adams," the inspector urged, but he obeyed Clint's command. "You're just making things worse."

"I don't see how that's possible." He glanced at Calley. The big cop still had Clint's gunbelt draped over a shoulder. "Take it off, put it on the floor and back off."

Calley obeyed. Clint hooked a foot around his gun-belt and pulled it closer. Watching the two policemen carefully, he gathered up the belt and buckled it around his lean waist.

"You fellas have handcuffs?" Clint inquired.

"Give it up, Adams," Kovac urged. "Running won't help you. You can't hide from the police in this city."

"If I can't use handcuffs to chain your hands behind your backs," Clint mused as he drew the forty-five from his hip holster, "I'll just have to knock you two unconscious. Don't fret. I'll try not to split anybody's skull. . . ."

"Give him the cuffs, Calley," Kovac said with a sigh.

Both policemen surrendered their handcuffs and keys. Clint told the pair to stand spread-eagle with their hands on the wall. Then he approached the pair from behind.

"Kovac," Clint said. "Lean your forehead against the wall and put your hands behind your back."

"You're crazy, Adams," the inspector declared, but he continued to follow orders.

Clint snapped a pair of handcuffs onto Kovac's wrists, binding the hands together at the small of his back. He turned to deal with Calley. The big cop had pivoted and suddenly lunged at Clint.

Calley's hands grabbed Clint's wrist behind the forty-five. He twisted hard and forced the Gunsmith to drop the pistol. Clint responded by hooking his left fist into Calley's jaw.

The cop staggered. Clint closed in fast and drove a right upper cut to Calley's solar plexus. The officer grunted as Clint followed up with another left hook. Calley blocked the punch with a forearm and tagged the Gunsmith on the jaw with a fast left jab.

Clint stepped backward with the blow and Calley threw a wild roundhouse right. The Gunsmith ducked under the attacking arm and slammed another punch to his opponent's battered solar plexus. Calley doubled up with a gasp.

The Gunsmith hooked a left under Calley's ribs. The cop convulsed in pain, but suddenly slashed a desperate backfist at Clint's face. The Gunsmith dodged the attack and delivered two fast jabs to the larger man, hitting him in the breastbone and the point of the jaw.

Calley swayed unsteadily, his eyes acquiring a glassy appearance. Clint plowed into his opponent and hit him once more in the solar plexus. The police officer uttered a strangled groan and wilted to the floor. The Gunsmith easily cuffed Calley's hands behind his back.

"I'm not going to have any trouble from you too, am I?" Clint asked as he glanced up at Kovac.

The inspector had raised his coattails behind his back and hooked both thumbs under his belt at the small of his spine. He looked at Clint and shrugged.

"Wouldn't do much good, would it?" Kovac said.

"You're a smart cop, Kovac," Clint commented as he scooped up his discarded Colt. "Carry a spare handcuff key under your belt just in case something like this happens, right?"

Kovac sighed. "How'd you know?"

"It's an old trick," the Gunsmith replied as he moved behind Kovac and fished the key out of its hiding place. "Got a handkerchief? Hate to gag you with a used sock."

"In my breast pocket," the inspector told him.

"Thanks." Clint plucked the cloth from Kovac's suit.

"What about Calley?" Kovac asked.

"He'll be okay after he gets his wind back," Clint explained. "Tough boy, even if he isn't very bright. I won't gag him, if that's what you mean. Fella might throw up and choke to death while he's unconscious if I gagged him."

"You'd better listen to me, Adams," Kovac began.

"Reckon I've heard enough to know I'm in a hell of a mess," Clint said. "And the police won't be much help at getting me out of it. Means I'll have to take care of things myself."

He tied the handkerchief around Kovac's jaw, with a knot lodged between the inspector's teeth. Clint gathered up his Springfield rifle and saddlebags and moved to the door. He listened to be certain no one was waiting outside his room. Carefully, he opened the door a mere crack.

The hall was empty. Clint slipped out and headed for the window at the end of the hall. There was a fire escape outside which allowed him to descend into an alley.

Where he would go and what he would do next, the Gunsmith had no idea.

Chapter Seven

John Chang and Sam Wing were startled when they entered their office and discovered the Gunsmith sitting in a chair with a carbine resting in his lap. Clint's right hand was on the frame, finger on the trigger guard, thumb on the hammer.

"What the hell?" Wing began. "How the hell did you get in here? The door was locked."

"I used a couple gunsmithing tools to pick the lock," Clint explained. "A thin metal probe and a narrow hacksaw blade. Wasn't very hard."

"I don't wish to be unpleasant," Chang said sternly, "but you have entered without permission. I trust you have an explanation."

"I need help and I don't know anyone else to turn to in this city," the Gunsmith told them.

"Well," Sam Wing said as he took out a pouch of tobacco and rolling papers, "you sure as hell know how to get our attention. Let's hear your story."

Clint told them what happened after he returned to his hotel room. Chang sat quietly with both index fingers pressed together, touching his lips as he listened. Wing crushed out his cigarette, shook his head and got out the whiskey bottle.

"You couldn't have gotten yourself in a worse situation if you raped the mayor's daughter in front of City

Hall at high noon," Wing muttered as he prepared to pour himself a drink. He noticed the whiskey level was lower than it had been the night before.

"Sorry." The Gunsmith shrugged. "I'll pay for a new bottle."

"Considering the situation," Chang remarked, "it is no wonder you found a stiff drink difficult to resist."

"Yeah," Wing muttered. "I guess we can relate to that. You know you can get us in a lot of trouble if the police find out you're here."

"I know that," Clint replied. "And I apologize for breaking in uninvited. It was rude, but necessary. I don't want to get you fellas involved, but I'd appreciate some information."

Wing shrugged. "Hell. We owe you for last night."

"Maybe," the Gunsmith replied. "But I'm not going to take unfair advantage of that. Just answer a couple questions about this Yellow Serpent Society, if you know anything about them, and I'll leave. Give me a couple hours before you contact the police. Fair enough?"

"If you're thinking of taking on the Yellow Serpents single-handed, forget it," Wing advised. "That would be like a terrier trying to fight a Bengal tiger."

"The Yellow Serpent Society is a Tong," Chang said. "In the fourteenth century an organization was created in China to fight the Mongol tyrants who then ruled the country. This was the White Lotus Society. It was a noble organization. Many Shaolin priests were members. They were quite successful and helped to overthrow the Mongols. Afterward a former Buddhist monk, Hung Wu, became emperor and the Ming Dynasty began. China once again belonged to the Chinese."

"But nothing lasts forever," Wing went on. "About three hundred years later the Manchus conquered China, but the White Lotus Society wasn't around anymore. It had split apart. Most of the old guard continued to be good, productive people. Others formed new societies. Some of these were okay too, but others became Tongs. These were—and still are—criminal organizations who deal in opium trade, white slavery, virtually anything that can make a dishonest profit."

"Some claim the Tong did this to raise money to finance a new revolution against the Manchus," Wing explained. "Perhaps they did, but they've certainly only been financing themselves for the last hundred years or so."

"And these Tong societies are here in America?" the Gunsmith asked.

"Oh, yes," Chang confirmed. "Especially here in San Francisco. There are several Tongs operating in this city. In the fifties there was a great power struggle among the different societies. Hatchet-wielding Tong enforcers fought in the streets. It is said blood flowed like rivers in the gutters."

"Some Tong outfits were wiped out," Wing added. "Others merged with more powerful societies. The biggest Tong societies call themselves the Five Companies after the five provinces of China. The Yellow Serpent Tong isn't big enough to be part of the Five Companies, but they're ambitious, vicious and all-around rotten bastards."

"The Yellow Serpent Tong is run by Mao Chu," Chang stated. "He's a ruthless man, cold-blooded and shrewd. It is said he is bitter about life and rules his Tong with an iron hand."

"And he's totally merciless with his enemies," Wing remarked. "Old Mao is the type who never stops looking for a fella when he has a score to settle. The only way to escape his revenge is to die before he finds you and even then his men will probably dig up your grave just to piss on your corpse."

"Where do I find this Mao Chu?" Clint asked.

"What are you planning to do?" Wing asked. "Call Mao out in the street? Meet him at high noon and shoot it out? This guy's no outlaw gang leader, Clint. He's a general with a small army of the worst killers you've ever seen. Tong assassins make your Texas outlaws look like Sunday school teachers."

"I've come up against some pretty clever fellers who had private armies before," Clint replied.

"But they weren't Tong," Chang told him. "You must realize that the Tong has a history older than this country. They operate differently than the Occidental criminals you've encountered in the past."

"People are people," the Gunsmith said. "Good or bad, they don't vary that much from one culture to another."

"Have you dealt with criminals who had their own code of honor?" Chang asked. "Who regard success of a task more important than their own lives? Who will kill themselves rather than lose face by failure?"

"As a matter of fact," the Gunsmith replied, "yes."

"No sense talking to this guy, John," Wing commented sourly as he rolled another cigarette. "He's bound and determined to tangle with Mao."

"Then we cannot allow him to face the Yellow Tong forces alone," Chang declared.

"What?" Wing stared at his partner. "Is insanity

contagious? Look, I don't want to turn my back on Clint either, but there's nothing we can do.''

"But we must," Chang insisted. "He is our friend. We will lose face if we refuse him help."

"And we'll lose our lives if we do help him," Wing said. "Or at least our detective license. Don't forget, the Yellow Serpents aren't our only problem here. The police are looking for Clint. We'll be lucky if they don't lock us up and ship the key to China."

"Sam's right," Clint stated as he rose from his chair. "I can't ask you to stick your neck out. Thanks for the information about the Tong."

"Wait a minute," Wing snapped. "Where the hell do you think you're going? We've got to figure out a safe place to put you until we get a chance to get in touch with a few of our contacts in the city. See what we can find out about the inner workings of the Yellow Serpent Tong. Maybe we can find somebody who will admit they knew this Su Li escaped from the brothel."

"It takes a few years to get used to Sam," Chang sighed. "And I don't think one ever really understands him, but he's not a bad sort."

"Are you two sure you want to do this?" Clint asked.

"Risking your life beats the shit out of losing face," Sam Wing declared as he poured himself another drink. "How's that for profound Chinese philosophy?"

"I'm stunned," Chang replied dryly.

Chapter Eight

The detectives hid Clint Adams in the back of their buggy and covered him with a blanket. They transported him to a house near the Line. The Gunsmith slipped out of the rig and joined Chang and Wing as they strolled to the house. Sam knocked on the door.

It opened and a pretty blond girl appeared in the doorway. She gazed up at Wing and smiled warmly. The young woman kissed both detectives on the cheek.

"I wondered when you two characters would show up on my doorstep again," she declared. "Come on inside."

Chang and Wing entered, followed by the Gunsmith. The girl raised her pale eyebrows when she saw Clint. He doffed his stetson and bowed formally. She nodded in reply.

"This is Amanda Lincoln," Chang said to the Gunsmith. "She's a good friend."

"But before we tell you about our round-eyed companion," Wing told the girl, "I think you'd better know he's in trouble. Lots of it."

"Criminal trouble"—she gave Clint a skeptical glance—"or trouble with the police?"

"Both," Chang replied. "The police arrested him last night and he was forced to escape. He came to us for help."

"What was he arrested for?" Amanda asked.

"Murder," the Gunsmith replied. "They think I strangled a Chinese girl in my hotel room."

"Oh." The woman nodded slowly.

"He was framed by the Yellow Serpents," Wing said. "You could get into trouble by having him under your roof, Amanda, but you don't have any reason to be afraid of him."

"Maybe you'd better explain this to me," the confused girl said.

The three men did so. The girl's mouth fell open when Clint admitted he had assaulted two police officers in order to escape. When they finished the tale, Amanda whistled softly.

"And you want him to stay here until you get a chance to check on some leads concerning the Yellow Serpent Tong?" Amanda asked.

"That's right," Sam Wing admitted. "If you refuse, we won't blame you. It is a hell of a risk."

"I always knew you two were crazy," she told the detectives. "I guess I am too. What's this guy's name?"

"Clint Adams, ma'am," the Gunsmith said.

"Any enemy of the Tong is a friend of mine, Clint," the girl stated. "Call me Amanda."

"Sam and I had better get to work," John Chang declared. "We'll be back tomorrow morning to see how you're doing."

"Okay," Wing added. "Make sure you take care about who you open that door for, Amanda. You and Clint sort of look after each other until we get back."

"We'll be careful," the girl promised. "Just make sure you take care too. I don't have to tell you what the Yellow Serpents are like."

"We'll be as careful as a priest sneaking out of a whorehouse." Wing grinned.

The detectives left the house. Amanda closed the door, locked it and threw the bolt into place. She then joined Clint in the sitting room.

"You look hungry," Amanda commented. "Want some lunch?"

"I don't want to be a bother," Clint told her. "Please don't go to any trouble on my account."

"No trouble," she assured him. "I'll fix some food. How does pork chow mein sound?"

"Never tried it, but I know what chow mein is. Some folks think it's Chinese food, but it really isn't. Chinese railroad workers in this country have a habit of taking leftovers and boiling it into a stew and that's where the name for chow mein really came from."

"True," Amanda replied. "But chow mein is becoming popular in San Francisco because a lot of the Chinese who were formerly railroad laborers have moved here."

"Do you have many Chinese friends?" Clint asked.

"What's that supposed to mean?" Amanda said defensively. "If you're referring to Sam and John, they've been friends ever since they caught my husband's murderer over a year ago. I have other Chinese friends—men and women. Do I sleep with Chinese men? Since my husband's death I've slept with only two men. One of them was Chinese—and he was terrific, by the way."

"Jesus Christ," the Gunsmith muttered. "I wasn't trying to pry into your personal life. I just wondered how well you know the Chinese population in the city."

"Sorry I overreacted," the girl said, her face

flushed with embarrassment. "Made a real fool of myself, didn't I?"

"You showed that you have a temper." Clint smiled. "Nothing wrong with that. I'm sorry about your husband."

"Harry owned a small import and sales business which specialized in buying and selling rice," Amanda explained. "He had it shipped up from the fields near Baja and sold it here. Most of his customers were Chinese. A splinter group of Tong enforcers decided this would be a good cover for their opium trade. When Harry refused to go along with the idea, they killed him.

"The police don't know how to deal with the Tong," she continued. "But John and Sam do. When I hired them, they said they'd do what they could and I'd only have to pay them the full fee if they found Harry's killers. They did. The Tong assassins were members of the Triad, the largest and most powerful of the Five Companies. John and Sam met with the Triad *ling-shyou* and told him some of his boys had done some moonlighting and murder on the side."

"What happened?" Clint asked.

"The *ling-shyou* brought the renegades into his assembly hall and asked if John and Sam told the truth. The Tong enforcers confessed immediately. The *ling-shyou* promptly had them executed. John and Sam actually watched as the renegades' heads were chopped off by a *shou-tao* sword. The Triad leader apologized for his men's conduct. Harry Lincoln had always been a friend to the Chinese, and the Tong appreciates whites who help Chinese."

"If they're so concerned about their people," Clint remarked, "why are they preying on them?"

"The Tong don't consider themselves criminals," Amanda explained. "They supply goods and services. There is a demand for opium and prostitution."

"Supply and demand," Clint said dryly. "How do they justify kidnapping, torture and murder as part of their version of free enterprise?"

"You're thinking like a civilized man, not a Chinese Tong. The United States of America has been a nation for little more than a hundred years. Since our revolution, we've had a constitutional republic which grants us freedoms and rights that no other country in the world offers.

"The Chinese, however, have an ancient culture," Amanda continued. "The Shang Ti period dates back almost fifteen thousand years. The Chinese are highly civilized, their arts are magnificent, their accomplishments and inventions too numerous to count. Yet, China has never had a free government."

"Yeah." Clint nodded. "I gathered that from a previous conversation with John and Sam. The Mongols ruled China for centuries before the Chinese reclaimed their own country. Then the Manchus took over. Sounds like they've either had a home-grown monarchy or a foreign dictatorship running the country for centuries."

"And the majority of the Chinese people have suffered under those tyrants," Amanda said. "The elite ruling class live in tremendous wealth and splendor while the masses are lucky to have a bowl of rice every day. If a peasant fails to bow deeply enough to an aristocrat, he can be killed on the spot. Starvation and oppression are commonplace. The lives of people in the lower class are not considered important by those in authority."

"So when the Tong decided to go into business," Clint began, "they had the attitude of these Chinese rulers as an example of how ambitious people acquire power and keep it."

"Exactly. Abducting a young girl for white slavery is the same as training a water buffalo to help harvest rice in the paddies. Murdering a poor Chinese is simply a practical way to dispose of a problem. However, the Tong renegades who killed Harry violated one of their codes. They killed a member of the white race which rules this country and a man who had become popular with the Chinese community. That's the only reason the Triad *ling-shyou* executed them."

"And because they were going into business for themselves and defying his authority," Clint added.

Amanda nodded. "Now you're beginning to understand how the Tong think."

"I also understand why they framed me for murder instead of killing me as well as Su Li," the Gunsmith said. "They don't want to attract attention from the police. If a white man kills a Chinese girl it doesn't bring the authority down on the Yellow Serpents' operations."

"But if you and Su Li had been found dead," Amanda added, "the police may have wondered about the girl. They may have found out she was from a brothel operated by the Yellow Serpent Tong."

"You're a smart lady." Clint grinned. "Can you cook as well?"

"Sure." She smiled. "I'd better get lunch ready."

Chapter Nine

Amanda served the pork chow mein with Chinese noodles and jasmine tea. The Gunsmith was more accustomed to meat, potatoes and coffee, yet he found the meal to be a very pleasant change of pace. The couple relaxed on the sofa in the sitting room after the meal. Amanda poured them each a glass of raspberry brandy.

"How have you managed since your husband's death?" Clint asked, glancing around the cozy, well-kept room.

"Not badly," she admitted. "I sold half of Harry's business to another importer. He handles the shipping and distribution while I arrange sales, especially with the Chinese. It's a fair deal and we both make a good profit."

"You're an impressive lady," Clint said, saluting her with the brandy glass.

"And you're an interesting man, Clint," Amanda replied. "You're intelligent, obviously educated in the East, yet you seem to have adjusted very well to the West. Sam told me you're unbelievable with a gun as well. From our conversations, I've also noticed you have a good insight into people."

"I'm flattered." The Gunsmith smiled.

"The truth shouldn't flatter you," Amanda said. "And I'm certain a handsome man like you has been complimented by women before."

"Once or twice." The Gunsmith grinned. "But I never get tired of hearing it. Especially from a beautiful lady."

"Seems that we admire each other quite a bit," Amanda said coyly, and leaning toward Clint she ran a hand along his thigh.

"Maybe," Clint said, as he drew Amanda closer, "we should do something about that."

Now they embraced, their mouths meeting in a fiery kiss. Their hands began to passionately explore each other's bodies. Clint's fingers deftly played along the girl's spine while Amanda unbuttoned his shirt and slipped her hands inside to caress his hairy chest.

Clint's lips moved to Amanda's neck. He kissed her tenderly, tickling her throat with his tongue. Amanda peeled off Clint's shirt while he fumbled with the buttons to her gingham dress.

"Why don't we move to the bedroom?" Amanda whispered, nibbling on Clint's earlobe.

"Because I don't know where the hell it is," the Gunsmith replied as he fondled her breasts, thumbing the stiff peaks of Amanda's erect nipples.

"Follow me," the girl said, patting the bulge at Clint's crotch.

Amanda led the way to a small, neat room with a large brass bed. He unbuckled his gunbelt and hung it over the headboard while Amanda stripped off her dress. Clint followed her example and soon both were naked.

Amanda's body was magnificent. Her breasts were perfectly formed, her body curved into a narrow waist and flared at the hips before tapering into long thighs and shapely legs. Amanda observed Clint's body with equal appreciation.

They moved to the bed and sprawled across the mattress. Their arms encircled each other. Lips moved from faces to neck. Clint kissed her breasts, gently teasing the nipples with his teeth. He sucked her lovely mounds and slid his hands along her soft flesh to her hips.

Amanda groaned as Clint stroked her with his skillful touch. He shifted his body and moved his lips to her belly. Clint's tongue traced a moist line down to her navel and then he continued down to Amanda's thighs. She trembled as Clint's tongue found the warm, damp triangle of her womanhood.

"Oh, God," Amanda gasped. "I'm ready whenever you are, darling."

Clint didn't need any more encouragement, and Amanda spread her legs wide to receive his stiff, hungry cock. She wrapped her legs around Clint's hips and hugged him firmly as he increased the speed and force of his thrusts. Soon Amanda exploded into a wild orgasm.

Clint resisted the urge to keep lunging until he could release his load as well. Instead he slowed his pace and slowly brought her to the brink a second time. When he felt Amanda's body buck and convulse once more, he rammed himself home, harder and faster. Together they burst into an erotic frenzy before they climaxed in unison.

Chapter Ten

John Chang and Sam Wing returned to Amanda's house the following morning. The girl welcomed them in and prepared breakfast for them all. Clint was relieved to see cups of coffee, bacon and eggs on the table. His American appetite didn't relish the idea of Chinese food first thing in the morning.

"Here's a cup of tea for you, John," she told Chang.

"You're still the most considerate person I know," Chang replied with a smile. "Thank you, Amanda."

"Uh-huh," Wing growled. "You remembered his tea but I bet you didn't put any whiskey in my coffee, did you?"

"You'll just have to rough it today," Amanda said, laughing.

"Should have brought my flask," Wing sighed.

"You are not going to carry that thing around when we're working on an investigation," Chang scolded.

"Save the lecture for later," his partner moaned. "We might have time to quarrel about it then."

"Did you guys find out anything last night?" the Gunsmith asked.

"We located a certain opium addict who does odd jobs for the Yellow Serpent Tong," Chang began. "For the price of a pipe full of opium, this man will tell anyone anything he knows."

"How reliable can an opium addict be?" Clint frowned.

"We've used him before," Wing answered, "and he's never given us false information. John and I sort of made an impression on him that scared him badly enough to guarantee truthful answers forever."

"You must have made a pretty nasty threat," Clint remarked.

"We simply gave him a demonstration of *wu-shu*," John Chang said with a shrug.

"I just broke a two-by-ten board with a *ming-chuan* punch," Wing explained. "Of course, John had to show off by throwing three clay jugs into the air, jumping up and breaking them with kicks before they could hit the ground."

"Three jugs?" Clint stared at Chang. "Christ, you must be fast."

"Don't give him a swelled head," Wing said. "Besides, it really isn't that good a trick. After all, the jugs would have broken anyway when they hit the ground. Right?"

"You guys are . . ." Clint couldn't find an apt description so just shook his head and grinned at them. "So what did this opium addict tell you?"

"When we asked if he knew about a young Chinese girl who recently escaped from one of the Yellow Serpent brothels," Chang began, "he said that he had not heard about it."

Clint couldn't repress a sigh of disappointment.

"But he did tell us," Chang continued, "that the Yellow Serpent Society only has one brothel. It isn't as large as the Five Companies."

"It's called the Flowers of Paradise," Wing added. "I know where it is. Know a couple of the girls who work there too."

"I'm sure you do," Amanda said dryly.

"Hey"—Wing held up his hands defensively—"I didn't know the place was run by the Yellow Serpents or that they forced girls into prostitution. A lot of women chose that profession of their own free will. . . ."

"We're not questioning your morals," Chang commented. "We all know you don't have any to speak of."

"Why don't you go sit in a corner and meditate or something?" Wing snorted.

"Where is this brothel?" Clint asked.

"It's located at the wharf," Wing answered. "Rough place. Lot of stevedores and sailors go there, but you'd be surprised by the number of high and mighty mucky-mucks show up as well. Sometimes it's fun just to watch all the big businessmen and city hall officials trying to hide from each other. It looks like an ostrich convention."

"Sounds like we've got a place to start looking for clues," the Gunsmith remarked.

"That's what John and I figured too," Sam declared, rolling a cigarette. "We plan to check it out tonight."

"But first we have to see Inspector Kovac at police headquarters," Chang added as he pulled a turnip-shaped pocket watch from his vest. "He left a note under our office door 'requesting' our presence."

"I can guess what he wants," Clint commented.

"If he asks about you"—Wing shrugged—"we'll just say we don't know anything. We never tell the police more than we want them to know anyway."

"When do we pay a visit to the Flowers of Paradise?" the Gunsmith wanted to know.

"You're planning to come with us?" Chang asked

with surprise. "I do not think that is wise."

"I'm not going to stay here and wait for you guys to come back," Clint said. "It isn't right that you take all the risks."

"With every bull in San Francisco looking for you," Wing said, "that makes as much sense as trying to fight a range fire by pissing on it."

"Who are the police looking for?" Clint asked. "They're looking for a man dressed in denim and a stetson hat with a six-gun on his hip. All I need is a change of clothing."

"What about that scar on your cheek?" Amanda observed. "I'm sure they have that mentioned in the description of you."

"There're ways to cover that up as well," the Gunsmith insisted.

"Very well," Chang agreed reluctantly as he put away his pocket watch. "Sam and I had better have our chat with the police inspector. We'll be back some time after noon. We can discuss our plan of action then."

Chapter Eleven

Sam Wing drove the horse and buggy through the streets of San Francisco as twilight fell. John Chang and a tall man with a mustache and muttonchops sat beside Wing. All three wore black cotton suits and derby hats.

"This hair on my face itches," Clint Adams muttered, resisting the urge to scratch the false mustache and sideburns glued to his skin.

"It was your idea," Wing commented as he tugged the reins gently to steer the one horse vehicle.

"Don't rub it in," the Gunsmith said with a sigh. "Something occurred to me. This opium addict who gave you information about this brothel can be bought for the price of a pipe dream, right?"

"Yeah," Wing said. "I hope you realize we won't charge you the usual fee for our services, but you will have to pay for our expenses after this is over. John and I aren't exactly independently wealthy, you know."

"That's no problem," Clint assured him. "But I'm worried about this opium addict. The Yellow Serpents probably know the guy can be bought for a few dollars. He doesn't sound like he's strong enough to keep his mouth shut if they ask him if anyone has talked to him about Su Li or me."

"That's true," Chang agreed. "Why does this worry you, Clint?"

"Because it will lead the Tong straight to you and Sam," the Gunsmith replied.

"Give us credit for a little intelligence," Wing said. "Hell, we've never told that opium puffing idiot who we really are. He thinks we're Tong enforcers from the Triad. If the Yellow Serpents question our little canary and hear that, they'll let the matter drop. Mao Chou knows better than to dishonor the Triad by questioning their motives for anything. No little Tong outfit ever messes with the Five Companies."

Clint watched a man prop a ladder against a street-lamp. The fellow mounted the rungs and lit the coal-oil lamp at the top of the tall, tin stem.

"Okay, gents," Wing began. "We're almost at the wharf. You guys remember the names of the girls I told you about?"

"Jennifer, Lyang Hwu and Yu-li T'Yan," Chang replied.

Sam nodded. "Right. Clint, you might have trouble pronouncing the Chinese names. If you get the voice tone wrong or mispronounce a single vowel, it can change the entire meaning of a word. Better ask for the girls by their Occidental translations—Bright Flower and Night Sky."

"I don't intend to go to bed with a whore," Clint told him.

"You plan to play chess in the lobby while we're upstairs?" Wing asked. "If you don't go up with a girl it'll look suspicious. The owners will probably figure we're all cops, or worse, they might even suspect who we really are."

"I could wait downstairs and claim I'm waiting for a

turn with one of the girls you two are with,'' the Gunsmith suggested.

"Very well," Chang said. "The girls would be more suspicious of you than they would be with two Chinese anyway. Just be very careful what you say to anyone inside the Flowers of Paradise. If this is a Tong establishment, none of us can afford to make any mistakes in there.''

The buggy approached the Flowers of Paradise as twilight dissolved into night. The building appeared to be an expensive waterfront hotel with Doric columns supporting the porch roof and iron-frame balconies jutting from the upstairs windows. There was no sign posted to inform passersby of the building's purpose.

The three men parked the buggy, tied the horse to a hitching rail, and walked to the building and up the front steps. A Chinese in formal attire met them at the door. He bowed deeply.

"*Hau bu hau, Wing-shun-shang,*" the man greeted when he recognized Sam.

Wing conversed briefly with the man in Cantonese. Clint stood silently, unable to understand a word. The man smiled broadly and bowed repeatedly as he backed away. Wing and Chang crossed the threshold so Clint figured he was supposed to as well.

"Mr. Wing informs me you understand English," the man told Chang and Clint. "I welcome you to Flowers of Paradise. Please make yourselves comfortable."

He led them into a spacious lobby which featured a crimson carpet and ivory frame furniture with felt seats and backrests. A pair of Oriental urns with colorful flowers painted on them flanked a doorway with a beaded curtain. A long stairway led to the next story.

"Shall I have some of our ladies come forward so you can make your selections," their host said. "Or do you have someone special in mind?"

"We're interested in three of my favorites," Wing replied. "Jennifer, Lyang Hwu and Yu-li T'Yan."

"Lyang Hwu is no longer employed here," the man answered. "The other two girls are available."

"You two go ahead," Clint announced, annoyed with Wing, who had obviously tried to get all three of them upstairs with the trio of girls. "I'll wait and hear what you have to say about them before I decide."

"As you wish, Mr. Jones," Chang told him. "Shall we go now, Sam?"

"I can hardly wait," Wing said as he bowed to his partner.

The host led the two up the stairs. The Gunsmith moved to one of the chairs in the lobby and sat, glancing about, admiring the place for its style. It certainly didn't look like a whorehouse. In fact, he found it difficult to believe stevedores and sailors would be attracted to the brothel.

As if to dispel Clint's doubts, a pair of grinning sailors clad in white uniforms descended the stairs. They stumbled drunkenly from riser to riser until they reached the bottom. One sailor grinned at Clint and winked as his partner pulled his sleeve to escort him to the door.

"Those two were not difficult to please," a woman's musical voice laughed.

The Gunsmith turned to see a tall Oriental woman emerge from behind the beaded curtain. Her raven black hair was fashioned into a crown, held in place by a diamond stickpin. Blue makeup highlighted her upper eyelids and she wore a light application of red rouge on her tempting full lips.

Her dress clung to her shapely, sleek body like a second skin. The Mandarin collar was high on her throat and her large, round breasts strained against the scarlet silk. The skirt was slit on both legs to above the knee.

Yet Clint noticed the unusual design on her dress as much as her splendid body. The symbol of a yellow serpent curled around red cloth.

"Apparently you're more difficult to satisfy than most of the men who come here," the woman told Clint with a coy smile. "Or perhaps you haven't seen anything of interest yet."

The Gunsmith smiled in return. "I have now," he assured her.

Chapter Twelve

"I'll take that as a compliment, Mr.—?" the girl asked.

"Just call me Jones," Clint replied. "What's your name?"

"No more honest than yours," she said, laughing. "I am known as Jade."

"Fair enough." The Gunsmith smiled. "You are indeed a beautiful and precious work of Chinese art, Jade."

"But I do not sell my body," she declared, gliding gracefully across the room to a chair across from Clint. "I am the manager and unofficial hostess of this establishment."

She sat down and smiled at the Gunsmith. Jade slowly crossed one leg over the other. The slit skirt offered Clint a lovely display of long shapely legs.

"Nice of you to come out and chat with the customers," Clint remarked, openly gazing over the Oriental beauty.

"I assure you I generally don't do this," Jade admitted. "But I have a feeling you are not just a customer, Mr. Jones."

The Gunsmith shrugged. "Far be it from me to argue with woman's intuition."

"A bit more than that," she declared. "You're wearing a false mustache and sideburns. You also have a revolver thrust in your belt under your jacket."

"You're very observant, Jade."

"I'm certain you are also, Mr. Jones," she replied, slowly uncrossing her legs. She dropped a hand into her lap before she recrossed her legs. From the amount of thigh Jade revealed, Clint suspected she'd purposely hiked her skirt up higher.

"I'm enjoying the show," he said frankly.

"Good." The girl nodded. "What do you do for a living, Mr. Jones?"

"I help people take care of special problems," Clint answered.

"By using a gun?" Jade raised an eyebrow.

"Maybe."

"Who do you work for, Mr. Jones?"

"I'm between jobs." Clint smiled.

"Looking for an employer?"

"Right now I'm just looking." The Gunsmith grinned wider and tilted his head at Jade.

"Let's talk about this in private, Mr. Jones," she suggested.

The girl rose and moved to the beaded curtain. Clint followed. He unbuttoned his jacket to allow rapid access to his pistol.

She escorted him into a corridor and directly to a white panel door. Jade opened it and led Clint inside a plush office with a thick carpet, teakwood furniture and a collection of hand-carved figures made of Chinese green jade. A bamboo birdcage hung from the ceiling contained two yellow canaries.

The girl closed the door and locked it. After glancing about the room to be relatively certain there was no threat lurking in the office, the Gunsmith took Jade gently by the shoulders and turned her slightly until they faced each other.

He kissed her fiercely, thrusting his tongue deep into her mouth, one hand behind her head, the other pressing against her breast. She slid her hands down the length of Clint's body and slipped one between his legs to massage his hardened manhood.

Clint caressed Jade's stiff nipples beneath the silk dress as she unbuttoned Clint's trousers to release his swollen penis.

The woman broke their embrace and slowly slid down Clint's chest and abdomen, lowering herself to one knee. Jade's lips parted and descended upon the Gunsmith's cock. She took him into her mouth, expertly slipping her lips over the head of his penis and sliding it slowly to the root.

She licked the length of his shaft as she cupped his testicles in one hand, fingers gently massaging.

"Jade," Clint whispered, trying to warn her that he was rapidly approaching the brink.

She ignored him and sucked harder, moving her head back and forth faster and faster. The Gunsmith moaned with pleasure when he finally released his load and poured hot semen inside Jade's mouth. Even then, she continued to suck, draining him as though trying to pump his balls flat. At last, Jade released him.

"Now we can concentrate on business for a few minutes," she commented.

"That's the only reason you did this?" the Gunsmith asked gruffly, buttoning his trousers.

"For now," she replied simply. "Take off that absurd disguise. You don't need it in here."

"Let's hear your offer first," the Gunsmith said. "I

may not be interested, which will mean you sucked me off for nothing.''

"Not quite nothing.'' She grinned.

Jade strolled over to the bird cage and gazed at the canaries as she spoke. "I trust you came here because you know about Mr. Mao, correct?"

"I've heard about him,'' Clint admitted.

"Then you know he's looking for white men of a suitable persuasion who will be loyal members of the Yellow Serpent Tong.''

"It has me curious,'' the Gunsmith said honestly.

Jade turned from the birdcage to face him. "You probably wondered about this story since the Tong has always been comprised of Chinese only.''

"That's what I've heard,'' Clint replied.

Jade moved to a cream-colored sofa and sat down, crossing her legs in her usual provocative manner. Clint crossed the room and sat beside her. The girl reached a hand to his face and gently pulled off one of the muttonchop sideburns.

"You're looking better, Mr. Jones,'' she remarked. "Or whoever you really are.''

She reached for the other sideburn, but Clint grabbed her wrist.

"Tell me why Mao wants white men in his Tong,'' the Gunsmith insisted.

"Because the Five Companies are too strong in San Francisco,'' Jade replied. "The Yellow Serpent Society cannot compete with them in this city. It is time to move on. It is time to operate beyond the confines of Chinatown and waterfront operations. Mr. Mao will need white Tong members if this is to be successful.''

"Your Mr. Mao is an ambitious man,'' the Gunsmith commented as he peeled off the other muttonchop and false mustache.

"Does this mean I've succeeded in capturing your interest?" Jade inquired.

"You sure have," Clint admitted, placing a hand on her knee.

"Mr. Mao will be here later this night," she stated, glancing down at Clint's hand as it slipped under the slit skirt to travel up her thigh.

"I hope he won't be here too soon," the Gunsmith said as he stroked her warm, smooth flesh.

"Not for another hour or two," Jade assured him.

"Good," he whispered. "That'll give us a little more time to get to know each other better."

Chapter Thirteen

The Gunsmith and Jade made love on the sofa. Yet, Clint realized, love had little to do with their sex. Su Li may have called this pillowing, but the Gunsmith considered this too gentle a term.

He couldn't be certain about Jade's motives, but he was driven by lust. Jade was a beautiful, sexy woman with a cold personality. She made love—or pillowed—with considerable skill. For Clint this was all that mattered as he blasted his seed between her beautiful long legs.

When they finished, Jade slid into her dress. She checked her appearance in a wall mirror while Clint pulled on his clothes.

"Wait here, Mr. Jones," she told him as she headed for the door. "Mr. Mao will see you when he arrives."

Twenty minutes later, the leader of the Yellow Serpent Tong entered the room.

Clint wasn't quite sure what to expect, but the small middle-aged Oriental dressed in a white linen suit didn't look like the boss of a ruthless criminal organization. His features were pasty and pale. His nose was flat with a long wisp of a mustache dangling from his upper lip.

Two young Chinese men accompanied the Tong leader. They could have been twin brothers. They wore the same funeral-black suit and derby. Both men were roughly the same size and age and both had the blank, expressionless face of a stone killer.

"I am Mr. Mao," the Yellow Serpent ringleader announced in fluent English with a surprising British accent.

"You can call me Jones." Clint bowed to show his respect for the Chinese.

"Jade may not object to such games," Mao said sternly, "but I have no intention of tolerating lies of any sort. Your real name, please."

"Warren Murphy," the Gunsmith declared, using the name of a professional gunfighter with a reputation that rivaled his own.

In fact, Clint had met Murphy, who was better known as the Irish Gun, on two occasions. The first time had been in Avalon, New Mexico where the two men had nearly drawn against each other. The second occasion had briefly united the pair as allies against a power-hungry rancher in Nevada.

As far as the Gunsmith knew, Murphy was still alive and selling his gun for profit. The Irish Gun, like Clint, was a drifter who moved from state to state in search of employment that suited his taste. His name seemed as good as any to use under the circumstances. Better than most.

Mao Chu nodded. "I've heard of you. Mr. Murphy. I understand you're supposed to be one of the top five gunfighters in the West."

"It's sort of hard to say who number one is until the other four are dead." Clint shrugged.

"A valid point," Mao said. "What do you think about working for a Tong society?"

"If I wasn't interested, I wouldn't be here."

Mao nodded. "Of course not. What is your usual fee, Mr. Murphy?"

"That's always depended on the job," Clint said. "How many men I'd have to go up against and what kind of fellas they happened to be."

"Indeed," Mao agreed. "Then you're not accustomed to a regular salary?"

"Doesn't happen often in my business," Clint replied.

"Good," Mao said. "Because you won't receive a regular salary from me either."

"What does that mean?"

"It means you'll work on commission," the Tong boss explained. "After all, this isn't Dodge City. Gunfights aren't standard practice here."

"I thought you planned to expand operations beyond San Francisco," Clint remarked.

"Certainly," Mao answered. "But we'll naturally set up future operations in cities similar to this one."

"When would I start work?"

"We'll put you on the payroll now." Mao turned to one of his Tong enforcers and said something to him in Chinese. The enforcer seemed surprised and stared at Clint.

"*Yi-kan djyow!*" Mao snapped.

"*Han hau*," the enforcer replied, bowing and nodding as he hastily backed toward the door.

"I just told Ho to get two thousand dollars from the vault," Mao explained. "Consider it a down payment, Mr. Murphy."

"That's a lot of money for an advance," Clint said.

"We're a successful organization and we pay well to insure loyalty." Mao shrugged. "Where are you staying at this time?"

"I don't have a place yet."

"We'll see to that," the Tong boss assured him. "Probably tuck you away out here by the harbor."

"That's mighty generous, Mr. Mao."

"Not at all. You are a professional, yes? Tell me, are you really as fast with a gun as the legends about you claim?"

"I'm still alive." Clint shrugged.

"Would you say that you're as fast as the Gunsmith?"

"He and I are probably pretty close," Clint replied, his stomach knotting up.

"I see." Mao nodded. "Did Jade treat you with proper hospitality?"

"Very much so," Clint replied.

"I'm so glad." Mao smiled thinly.

Ho returned to the office. The Tong enforcer stepped forward and pointed a Greener shotgun at the Gunsmith. Clint stiffened when he stared into the twin barrels of the scattergun.

"Do not attempt to draw your pistol," Mao warned. "You'll never make it, Mr. Adams."

Chapter Fourteen

Mao Chu snapped an order to his other Tong body-guard. The man nodded and hurried forward. Taking care not to step in front of Ho's shotgun, the enforcer moved beside Clint Adams and pulled the modified forty-five Colt from the Gunsmith's belt.

"Congratulations, Mr. Mao," Clint said as he raised his hands in surrender. "How'd you figure out who I really am?"

"I read the newspapers, Mr. Adams," Mao replied. "You fit the description of the Gunsmith. The right height, build and of course the scar on your cheek. You should have kept your disguise on, Mr. Adams."

"Jade realized the mustache and sideburns weren't real," Clint stated.

"She has a keen eye," Mao remarked. "Of course, she didn't know you'd claim to be Warren Murphy. That was a mistake, Mr. Adams. I'm surprised you decided to stay in San Francisco. Why didn't you leave the city when you had the chance?"

"And be labeled a murderer?" Clint shook his head. "No way, fella. Besides, that girl came to me for help. I failed to protect her so I've got a responsibility to see to it her killers pay for their crime."

"Such lofty moral convictions from a gunfighter,"

Mao said with amusement. "You're a complex man, Mr. Adams."

"I'm not a gunfighter," Clint replied. "And only an immoral hootowl like you would fail to understand why I want to see your rotten organization come crashing down."

"You won't even see the sunrise, Mr. Adams."

"Why'd you kill Su Li?" the Gunsmith asked. "She wasn't a threat to you."

"She was my property." Mao shrugged. "I could kill her if I wished. She was of no importance except for how she could serve my business interests."

"She was a human being," Clint insisted.

"Human beings are commodities," Mao replied. "Items to be used for goods and services. They belong to whoever can use their petty little talents to make a profit. The girl had a roof over her head. She was fed and clothed and if she was punished for rebellious behavior, that was her own fault."

"Why didn't you just let her go if she was so unimportant?"

"Would a rancher allow his cattle to stray?" Mao asked. "Would he allow a thief to steal them? Certainly not. He would hang a cattle rustler who stole his property. The girl made a decision to leave. Thus, she was both cattle and rustler. I ordered her execution just as a rancher would deal with our figurative thief. There is no difference."

"Christ, that's crazy," Clint spat angrily.

"Mr. Adams," Mao said, "do you know why criminals are executed by societies? It is not to punish them as much as to use that individual for an example to others. A warning of the price for failing to obey the rules of society. If I allowed the girl to escape unpunished, others may have decided to leave the brothel as well. An example had to be made."

"How does a man sink to your level?" the Gunsmith asked. "How can you have such contempt for human life?"

"Human life." Mao shook his head. "Let me tell you about human life. Thousands of starving people who have become animals due to desperation. Emperors who live in unbelievable luxury and find it entertaining to watch their court torturers perform the Death of a Thousand Cuts. Have you ever seen a man tortured to death for entertainment? Have you ever listened to a man scream for an entire day and a half? Have you seen the torturers slice off more and more of a victim's flesh?"

"So the tyrants in China are assholes," Clint said. "I figure that gives you an excuse to follow their example?"

"I'm telling you about life, Mr. Adams," Mao replied. "Human life which is of such little value that men are killed for a bowl of rice. The peasant class is no better than the aristocrats. Parents sell their daughters to brothels for a few shillings. They beg the royalty to take their newborn infant sons. You see, the parents are paid for their sons—providing the boy survives castration. The Manchu elite prefer their male servants to be eunuchs. Sometimes the parents even castrate their sons personally.

"That's the value of human life, Mr. Adams," Mao declared savagely. "It's worth only what one can get for it. Otherwise, it consists of unprincipled scum. The wise seize power while the ignorant suffer for their lack of ambition. In the end, the powerful are buried in fine tombs with monuments to honor their achievements.

The poor become corpses floating down the Yang Tzu river, merging into piles to form islands of decay.''

"And you'd rather be an emperor than a peasant?" Clint inquired.

"Of course, Mr. Adams." Mao smiled. "One is either master or slave. No rational man would chose the latter. Yet most men lack the drive, the determination and the utter ruthlessness required to claim power. I do not moralize, Mr. Adams. Morality is stupidity. It consists of rules and standards conceived by the ruling class to keep their subjects in line. The emperors and kings don't follow these codes themselves. Corruption is part of the world. I did not make it such. I merely accept it.''

"It's men like you who breed that corruption," the Gunsmith told him.

"Perhaps." The Tong leader nodded. "But we couldn't thrive on corruption if it wasn't part of man's nature. This debate is leading nowhere, Mr. Adams. It is time to dispose of you before you make a pest of yourself.''

"Let me guess," Clint began. "You're going to kill me and turn my body over to the police and say I tried to break into the Flowers of Paradise in order to strangle another girl?''

"Hardly," Mao replied dryly. "When Ming Chuan and Shin Chi arranged for you to take the blame for Su Li's death, allowing the police and the courts to take care of you was a sound plan. The Tong would not be involved. Now, the best that can happen—from my point of view—is for the notorious Gunsmith to simply disappear. You will vanish, Mr. Adams. Only your legend will remain after tonight.''

He spoke to his enforcers in rapid Chinese. The Tong members nodded in agreement. Clint wondered if he could manage to get his New Line hideout gun out of his shirt and put a twenty-two round between Mao Chu's beady eyes before the goon with the shotgun could blow his head off. The Gunsmith realized that was desperation tugging at his thoughts. *Calm down,* he told himself. *You're not dead yet.*

"I've just instructed Ho and Chu to take care of you, Mr. Adams," Mao announced. "You will be taken outside to the pier. Death will be quick. I have no desire to make you suffer. In fact, I rather admire you. You're a clever, resourceful man. You could have achieved much if you didn't allow your morality to block your progress."

"You mean I could have grown up to be just like you?" Clint snorted. "Don't be insulting, Mao."

"You should thank me, Mr. Adams," Mao declared. "You will not die in a dirt road with an empty stomach or suffer the agonies of a torturer's knife. You will die swiftly from strangulation. Chu is quite good at that. It will be silent and quick. Then your corpse will be weighted down with chains and you'll receive a burial at sea. Really quite civilized."

"You shouldn't use terms you don't understand, Mao," the Gunsmith remarked.

"I've enjoyed our conversation," Mao stated as he rose from his chair. "But I have other things to see to. I must leave now."

The Tong leader headed for the door. He turned and smiled at the Gunsmith.

"Good-bye, Mr. Adams," Mao said. "May you rest in peace."

Chapter Fifteen

Ho and Chu escorted the Gunsmith into the corridor at gunpoint. Clint marched through the hallway with the hard muzzles of the twelve-gauge Greener jammed against his spine. They approached a door with a wooden bolt securing it.

"Ting-lo!" one of the Tong snapped as he shoved Clint into the door.

"Yeah," the Gunsmith muttered. "Fuck you too."

He guessed that the Chinese wanted him to stop and open the door. Clint threw back the bolt and pulled the door open. The cool salty breeze of the night air riding in from the ocean brushed Clint's face. The sensation would have been pleasant under different circumstances, but at that moment the breeze felt clammy, like the breath of the Grim Reaper.

The Tong hoodlums shoved Clint through the doorway. He stumbled into a wooden handrail and gazed down at the water. In the darkness the ocean appeared black and sinister, like the opening to a bottomless pit.

"Dung, wa-pu-tan!" a Tong enforcer snapped, pushing Clint along the plankwalk to the edge of the pier.

The Gunsmith staggered off balance and fell into the rail once more. He dropped his arms and slipped his right hand inside his shirt. Fingers touched the walnut grips of the Colt New Line pistol.

"Bu hau!" a voice snarled as the shotgun poked against Clint's back.

The Gunsmith suddenly whirled. His left forearm slammed into the barrels of the Greener, knocking the twin muzzles clear of his body. The scattergun boomed. Buckshot splintered wood and pelted the water beyond.

Clint quickly jammed the barrel of his New Line under the jaw of the startled Chinese. Ho's eyes opened wide in terror and astonishment as he realized what was about to happen. A shred of a second later, Clint fired the diminutive Colt and a twenty-two-caliber bullet burned through the soft flesh at the hollow of Ho's jaw, sizzled through his tongue and drilled its way through the roof of his mouth into Ho's brain.

Chu, the other Tong enforcer, swung the Gunsmith's own modified forty-five Colt toward Clint. The little New Line pistol spat fire twice. Bullets smashed into Chu's face before he could trigger the Colt. One round split a cheekbone while the other pierced Chu's left eyeball. Blood gushed from the socket as the Chinese thug staggered backward. He fell to the plankwalk, the forty-five slipping from his lifeless fingers.

"You guys were lousy tour guides," the Gunsmith rasped as he scooped up his modified Colt revolver.

"Lan-djow na-gu ran!" a voice cried from the brothel.

"Oh, shit," Clint hissed as three more Tong enforcers dashed toward him.

With the forty-five Colt in his right fist and the twenty-two New Line in his left, the Gunsmith stood his ground. One Tong soldier stopped to work the lever action of a Winchester carbine, another pointed a pistol at Clint while the third waved a short handled hatchet overhead. The Gunsmith immediately determined the pistolman to be the greatest threat. He shot the man in the chest, blasting a forty-five slug through his heart.

The hatchet-wielding opponent suddenly threw his weapon at Clint. The Gunsmith was caught off guard by the tactic and barely managed to weave his head in time to avoid the whirling hand-axe. The hatchet sailed over the handrail and dropped into the ocean with a subtle splash.

The Chinese rifleman aimed his gun at Clint while the third man boldly attacked Clint with his bare hands and feet. The Gunsmith fired his forty-five at the rifleman. The Tong goon's face burst into a crimson pulp as his arms shot overhead, tossing the Winchester into the water.

The third man closed in fast, moving in a sideways shuffle, hands held in a defensive *wu-shu* position. The Gunsmith wasn't about to fight the man hand to hand. He shot him in the chest with the twenty-two New Line, pumping the last two rounds into the martial artist.

The Tong hootowl kept coming and lashed a desperate sidekick at Clint's torso. The Gunsmith hammered the butt of his forty-five across the man's ankle and stopped the kick before it could connect. A hand slashed out in an attempt to chop Clint in the throat. It missed. The Chinese fell to the plankwalk, landing on his rump in an abrupt sitting position. He glanced down at the twin streams of crimson that dribbled from the bullet wounds in his chest. The man seemed to sigh. Then he sprawled on his back and accepted the fact he was dead.

The Gunsmith prepared to escape when he saw half a

dozen Tong enforcers jog from the Flowers of Paradise with an assortment of weapons in their hands.

"Jesus," Clint gasped. "They must turn these guys out on a printing press!"

There was no cover available except the corpses of the five men Clint had already killed. He only had three shells left in his Colt and the New Line bellygun was empty. He couldn't win against so many opponents under such conditions. Clint's only chance was to dive into the ocean and hope he could swim to safety before the Tong could locate him.

The Gunsmith was about to leap over the handrail when a new commotion erupted among the Tong attackers. He turned to see that John Chang and Sam Wing had joined the ruckus. The detectives had hit the unsuspecting Tong from behind and taken out two Chinese hoodlums before they knew what hit them.

The remaining four Tong enforcers turned to face the detectives. Chang closed in rapidly and delivered a high kick to an opponent's face. His heel crashed under the man's jaw, shattering bone on impact. Another Tong member swung a hatchet at Wing. The detective ducked under the murderous blade and rammed a fist into his assailant's crotch. The man dropped his hatchet and doubled up in agony. Wing slammed the side of his hand into the Tong's right temple and the man collapsed without a sound.

A Chinese hoodlum aimed a pistol at Sam Wing. Clint's Colt snarled. A slug crashed into the back of the man's skull, tore through his brain and blasted a gory exit hole from the center of his face. His corpse fell, the unfired gun still clenched in his fist.

The last Tong soldier swung a rusty cap-and-ball revolver toward the Gunsmith. Chang suddenly appeared beside him. The detective chopped the edge of his hand across the hoodlum's wrist. Bones popped. The man screamed and dropped his weapon. Chang's hand shot out to spear the hard tips of rigid fingers into the Tong's throat. The man staggered backward and fell to one knee. He clawed at his throat as if trying to put his crushed windpipe back together again. He failed. Blood spewed from his open mouth and he slumped lifeless at the feet of the detective.

"Thank God you guys showed up," the Gunsmith declared as he jogged forward to join Chang and Wing. "The odds were getting pretty bad."

"They're still not very good," Sam Wing replied gruffly as he pulled his forty-four S&W from its shoulder holster. "Let's get the hell out of here."

"Occasionally," Chang said, his unflappable calm still intact, "even Sam can say something that makes sense."

Chapter Sixteen

"We wondered what happened to you back there," Sam Wing told Clint after the trio had returned to the detectives' office.

"We came downstairs and you were gone," John Chang added. "We looked about for you inside as much as we could without attracting unwanted attention. When that didn't work, we went outside. After a bit, we heard shooting and ran to the back of the building. You know the rest."

"Well, the opportunity looked promising for a while." Clint sighed. "I really thought Mao was going to hire me until his man came into the room with a shotgun."

"We told you about Mao Chu," Chang commented. "Very shrewd, very ruthless."

"And cool," Clint stated. "He didn't bat an eye while he sat there asking me about what I thought about working for his Tong. He didn't give any hint that he knew who I was until his man had the drop on me. A real iceman."

"And he doesn't believe in taking any big chances," Wing commented. "He sure brought enough men with him for protection. The place was crawling with Tong."

"What bothers me the most about the guy is his

twisted logic," the Gunsmith said. "I've never met anyone who was so bitter. He really hates the entire world and genuinely believes he's right and everybody else is wrong. Mao thinks he has as much right to deal in opium, white slavery and murder as a rancher has to grow grass, feed his herd and sell the cattle to be butchered."

"Jade sounds more like my type," Wing joked. "She might be another cold fish, but at least she's decorative. Never saw her in the Flowers of Paradise. You say she's the manager and hostess?"

"*Unofficial* hostess," the Gunsmith corrected. "I guess that means she only comes out when she feels it's important. Wonder if she's Mao's mistress."

"She'd be a pretty frustrated one if she is," Wing remarked.

Clint raised his eyebrows in puzzlement.

"What Sam means is the woman can't be a mistress in the conventional sense because sex is out of the question for Mao Chu," Chang explained. "You see, before Mao came to the United States he was a servant to the court of the Manchu royalty."

"You mean he's a eunuch?" the Gunsmith asked. "Castrated as an infant? That explains a lot. I can understand some of his bitterness now."

"It explains more than that," Chang stated. "The Manchus employ castration because they believe it makes a servant more trustworthy. However, cutting off a man's testicles doesn't mean his ambition has been removed as well. Yet, many members of royalty have granted their eunuchs incredible power and authority. Eunuchs have become top advisors and aides in China. Many are quite shrewd and ruthless. Mao Chu is a classic example of this."

"We're going to get a classic example of Tong vengeance too," Wing commented as he began to pace the floor. "We killed a number of Mao's men tonight. He'll be after us now. *All* of us. It won't be hard to figure out that John and I helped you, Clint. The goddamn doorman knows who I am so it won't take any brilliant deductions to know John was with me."

"True," Chang agreed. "Mao will have to punish us for tonight or he'll lose face with his followers and himself."

"Christ, what a mess," Clint groaned. "Sorry I got you two into this. . . ."

"We volunteered, remember?" Wing said.

"Sam is right," Chang added. "We knew the risks when we agreed to help you. What matters now is how can we best combat the Yellow Serpent Tong?"

"Talking to those girls didn't help much," Wing said. "Jenny was good in bed, as always, but she didn't know anything about Su Li."

"Or she wouldn't talk if she did," Clint commented.

"The woman I spoke with wasn't any more useful," Chang said. "She knew Su Li had been killed, but she seemed to believe you did it, Clint."

"Well"—Wing shrugged— "at least we all got our shovel cleaned. Oh, the price of the prostitutes is included among our expenses, Clint."

"That's the least of my worries," the Gunsmith replied. "Wait a minute. Mao said something that might be useful. He mentioned the names of the two men who broke into my hotel room and murdered Su Li."

"Can you remember what their names were?" Chang asked.

"Ming Chu . . . something like that," Clint replied. "And Shin Chi . . . I think that was it."

"Shin Chi." Wing rolled his eyes toward the ceiling. "I don't believe it. That little weasel working for the Yellow Serpent Tong? That's like a rabbit hanging around with a nest of rattlesnakes."

"You know who he is?" Clint asked.

"He's a burglar," Wing answered. "Started out as a pickpocket and moved on to breaking and entering. He's always been a small-timer. No guts. If he was carrying a gun the night he broke into your room, it's probably the first time he ever held one. You did him a favor when you knocked him out before he could draw that pistol. Dumb bastard probably would have shot himself in the foot."

"Ming Chuan," Chang announced. "Was that the other man's name, Clint?"

"Yeah." The Gunsmith nodded. "Do you know who he is too?"

"Ming Chuan is a *wu-shu* expert," Chang explained. "He used to work as a bare-knuckle fighter on the Barbary Coast. *Ming Chuan* is the term for the Chinese *wu-shu* 'ram's head' punch. Unlike Occidentals, we use the big knuckles of the index and middle finger when we punch. This is much more powerful than a Western punch. Ming Chuan proved this in the ring. He was banned from boxing because he killed several pugilists. No one wanted to fight him."

"I remember Ming Chuan now," Wing declared, rolling a fresh cigarette. "*Chuan-shu* stylist. Did a couple demonstrations when he first came to San Francisco. Did a lot of breaking techniques. Ramming his fist through a stack of tiles, breaking three or four bricks with the side of his hand, that sort of thing."

"Four bricks with one blow of his hand?" Clint asked, stunned by the idea that a man could wield such power with his bare hand. "I once tangled with a prize fighter who hit like a mule, but even he couldn't have done something like that."

"Ming Chuan can," Wing assured him. "I've seen it. If he'd wanted to kill you the other night, he could have split your skull like a ripe melon."

"Jesus," the Gunsmith whispered.

"Boards and bricks don't hit back," Chang remarked, clearly unimpressed by Ming Chuan's prowess.

"Neither do people when they're hit that hard," Clint replied. "If I ever see that son of a bitch again, I'm going to put a bullet in his shiny bald head before he can get close enough to lay a finger on me again."

"Well," Wing began as he located his whiskey bottle, "Ming Chuan seemed to drop out of sight a while back. Now we know where he went. He'll be a tough character to find. Shin Chi ought to be a lot easier—if he hasn't gone underground."

"You think he's hiding?" Clint asked.

"I mean underground like six feet under it," Wing explained. "If the Tong just wanted him for one job, they've probably killed the poor bastard by now."

The sound of a fist pounding on the office door startled all three men. Clint and Wing immediately pulled their pistols from leather. Even Chang, who didn't like to use firearms except in a dire emergency which required more than martial arts to get out of, reached for his gun.

"Open up," a voice called through the door. "Inspector Kovac, police."

Chapter Seventeen

"Oh, shit," Clint Adams rasped. "Do you have a fire escape?"

"No," John Chang answered. "Hide under my desk."

The Gunsmith frowned, but he couldn't think of an alternative. Clint scrambled to the desk and slipped under it while Sam Wing moved to the door. Wing waited until the Gunsmith was hidden, ignoring Kovac's persistent knocking.

"Goddamn it," the police inspector snapped, "I know you're in there."

"Just a second," Wing said as he unlocked the door. He opened it. "Happy?"

"Want to make me happy, Sam?" Kovac asked as he entered the room. "You can shut up until I ask you some questions—and then you'd better answer them."

"Nice to see you too, Inspector," Wing said dryly. "I was just about to have a drink. I'd offer you one, but I know you're on duty."

"Good evening, Inspector," John Chang said quickly before his partner and Kovac could verbally butt heads. "May we help you?"

"For your sake, you'd better," Kovac replied. "What do you know about the Gunsmith?"

"Need work done on your pistol again?" Wing remarked as he poured whiskey into a glass. "You shouldn't tuck it into your trousers, Kovac. It might get rusty when you wet your pants."

"You shouldn't be rude to our guest," Chang insisted.

"No problem," Kovac assured him.

Clint heard glass shatter on the floor. Shiny slivers scattered under the desk. He clenched his teeth and braced his hunched back against the modesty panel. Pain lanced up from his right leg. A shard of glass had pierced his calf.

"Isn't he tough, John?" Wing asked. "The inspector just slapped my drink out of my hand. Bet he hits his wife the same way. Don't you, Kovac?"

"Inspector," John Chang said sharply as he perched a haunch on the edge of his desk. Clint felt the furniture move slightly. "You've come in here uninvited with a surly attitude. Now you've made a mess for us to clean up after you leave. As for the Gunsmith, your question is absurd. We've already talked about Clint Adams. We told you everything we know about the man."

"The inspector might not remember," Wing said. "After all, that conversation was this morning, more than twelve hours ago."

"I'm surprised somebody hasn't sewed your mouth shut, Wing," Kovac hissed.

"Take off your badge and try it," Wing invited.

"Inspector," Chang said, "we met Clint Adams at the Red Bull Saloon. He helped us when we arrested Charlie Madrid. He came down to the stationhouse and explained his role in the incident. Sam and I liked Mr. Adams. He seemed like a very fine man."

"He strangled a young Chinese girl," Kovac declared.

"We find that hard to believe, Inspector," Chang replied. "Perhaps because Mr. Adams saved our lives at the saloon."

"Okay, John," Kovac began. "I'm not so sure he's guilty myself. Sure he ran, but I guess we were a little hard on him. The evidence seemed mighty strong at the time and Adams's story didn't seem to make sense. I'm not so sure anymore."

"What changed your mind, Kovac?" Wing asked. "Did the department get its Ouija board fixed?"

"The inspector is trying to be civilized, Sam," Chang stated. "Let us respond in kind."

"Okay." Wing sighed. "Sorry, Kovac."

"I didn't say I changed my mind," the inspector declared, "but I will say there's room for doubt. When the dead girl was examined we found numerous scars, probably the result of whippings and cigarette burns. These were old scars. Adams didn't do it to her. Now, she was a whore at the Flowers of Paradise. Could be they mistreated her pretty badly and she really did escape from there, like Adams said."

"Have you talked to the people at this establishment?" Chang asked.

"They deny that the girl ever worked there. Claim they never heard of Su Li before."

"Think they'd admit it?" Wing inquired.

"Oh, we know she worked there. One of our officers remembered her from one of his social visits to the place. Try using that for evidence."

"What do you want from us, Inspector?" Chang asked.

"Adams may come to you two for help," Kovac answered. "He's been to San Francisco before, but that was a while back. Hasn't been back since his pal Hickok was killed. He might have other contacts in the city, but if I was in his place, I'd come to you guys."

"If you're ever accused of strangling a girl we'll be glad to see you," Wing stated. "What would you want us to do for you if that happened? Turn you over to the police?"

"If you know where Adams is," Kovac answered, "that's what you'd better do. Unless you two want your license pulled."

"If he contacts us," Chang said, "we'll suggest he turn himself in. We can't promise he'll follow our advice and we won't arrest him and turn him over to you. We owe him for the other night."

"I understand." Kovac sighed. "Do you two happen to know anything about a ruckus at the Flowers of Paradise tonight?"

"What sort of ruckus?" Chang asked.

"We think a big gunfight broke out at the pier. Story was that a whole bunch of men were killed. A paddywagon full of policemen went down there to check it out. There'd been a shooting. Lots of bullet holes, buckshot chewed up some wood and such, but only a little blood and no bodies. A tall Oriental woman, a real looker I'm told, explained that a drunken stevedore stumbled out back and shot up the pier. The bouncers supposedly fired a few shots in the air and scared the guy off. We can't prove anything else happened."

"What do you think happened?" Wing asked.

"I don't know," Kovac admitted. "But it's possible Clint Adams went there trying to find evidence to clear himself of a murder charge. If he did, you know as well as I do that he won't have a chance. Taking on the Yellow Serpent Tong is suicide. If you two help him, it'll be a funeral for three in the end."

"We'll bear that in mind if we see Mr. Adams," John Chang declared.

"Sure hope you fellas don't do anything stupid," Kovac remarked.

"Next time we won't let you in," Wing commented.

"Where's your broom?" Kovac asked. "I'll sweep up that glass."

"Forget it, Inspector," Chang said. "We will."

"Okay," Kovac said. "You two be careful."

Clint heard the door open and close.

"He's gone, Clint," Chang said softly. "But you'd better stay hidden for a couple more minutes."

"Just looked out the window," Wing said. "There's a couple bulls in plain clothes across the street."

"Keep the curtains closed," Chang told him.

"Of course I will," Wing growled. "What kind of idiot do you think I am?"

"After all these years," Chang replied, "I still haven't figured that out yet."

"Can I come out now?" the Gunsmith asked.

"It ought to be okay now," Wing answered. "But you'd better stay in the office until morning. The police will probably watch the place the rest of the night."

"It'll actually be safer to leave in the morning," Chang added. "The police will assume you'll do most of your movement under cover of darkness."

"Any idea what we'll do then?" Clint asked.

"We try to find a little sneak thief named Shin Chi," Wing replied. "And hope the Tong hasn't gotten to him first."

Chapter Eighteen

The Gunsmith had never actually been to Chinatown before. As he walked through the streets of the Chinese ghetto, he was stunned by the remarkably different culture. Signs bearing legends in Chinese ideographs were everywhere. The aroma of fried rice and boiled tea mingled with the stench of raw fish and human sweat. The streets were remarkably neat. The Orientals who strolled by wore freshly washed if faded clothing. The sweat was the result of honest labor.

Then John Chang and Sam Wing escorted Clint to another part of Chinatown. A collection of rundown shanties and ill-kempt boardinghouses. The Gunsmith shook his head when he saw the ugly side of Chinatown.

"Most of these people are opium addicts," Chang explained. "Chinese have their riffraff just like any other race, but you'll find less of it among them than you will in the white sections."

"But some of the riffraff here is worse," Wing added. He pointed to a small group of shanties surrounded by barbed wire. "Notice how that section is segregated from the rest?"

"Yeah." Clint nodded. "They've got a good three or four city blocks between those shacks and the other buildings."

"With good reason," Chang answered. "The people inside are lepers."

Clint stared at the detective. "You mean that literally?"

"Yes." Chang nodded. "The other Chinese in the community bring baskets of food and place it at the gate of the fence. The lepers are too disfigured and maimed to work. Their skin peels off, sometimes fingers and toes even drop off. This is the best existence they can have, here among their fellow sufferers."

"God, that's terrible," Clint said.

"It could be worse," Wing replied. "Leprosy isn't a highly contagious disease. Limited association is safe enough. When a leper dies, his body is placed at the edge of the fence. Naturally, the corpse must be burned. When the last leper dies, the shanties will be burned to the ground. The disease will no longer be a threat then."

"What about the poor devils who have to live with leprosy?" Clint asked. "Isolated from the rest of the world, watching their bodies rot away . . . Jesus, how they must suffer."

"Life can be very cruel," Chang agreed. "Perhaps this is a lesson to the rest of us to appreciate our healthy bodies and make the most of the opportunities we have. Fate is mysterious. Some questions can never be answered."

"You see what I go through, Clint?" Wing remarked. "You make a simple statement and John winds up giving you a philosophical fact."

"Let's just concentrate on finding Shin Chi," the Gunsmith suggested.

The trio checked two boardinghouses without finding the elusive thief. The third boardinghouse was a charm. After the detectives questioned the manager and handed him five dollars, the landlord told them that Shin Chi had been a tenant and showed them a register to prove his claim. The Gunsmith waited patiently, unable to understand the conversation in Chinese, depending on occasional translations to know what was being said. At last, Wing turned to Clint and explained the conversation in detail.

"Shin Chi checked out of this cockroach paradise two nights ago," Wing said. "The same night he and Ming Chuan broke into your room and killed Su Li."

"Shit," the Gunsmith muttered. "We're back where we started."

"Not quite," the detective explained. "The landlord happened to be in a tavern called the Dragonfly last night and guess who he saw? Shin Chi was in there chatting with the bartender. He also saw Shin Chi slip the bartender some cash before the guy showed our little thief a door to the storage room."

"So Shin Chi is probably hiding out at this Dragonfly tavern," Clint remarked.

"Or the bartender may be able to lead us to wherever the little shit is." Wing nodded. .

"At least we know the Tong hasn't caught up with him," Chang added. "Although I wonder if they have a reason for leaving Shin Chi alive."

"I've thought of that too," Clint said grimly. "The Yellow Serpents could have easily disposed of Shin Chi immediately after he served his purpose by breaking into my room. Maybe they're using him for bait."

"Which means we could be walking into a trap at the Dragonfly," Wing commented. "Guess we'll just have to go there and find out."

Chapter Nineteen

The Dragonfly Tavern was only a couple blocks from the slum. It was a shabby little saloon with windows tinted by smoke and fly dung. The red dragonfly emblem on the sign outside was faded and cracked. As Clint and the detectives approached the entrance, they smelled dust and sweat and puke.

Inside was a small barroom with apple crates for chairs and square boards mounted on beer kegs for tables. Four musclebound Chinese stevedores sat around one table, drinking beer and playing poker with matchsticks. A squat, fat Oriental leaned against the crude counter, smoking a long-stemmed pipe. The sweet odor of the smoke told Clint the fellow didn't have tobacco in the pipe bowl.

"You the bartender?" Wing asked, noticing the fat man's apron.

"What do you think, fella," the barman replied in broken English, smiling at the detective.

"You must be the bartender," Wing remarked. "Doesn't look like you've got a maid working here."

"You want drink or you want talk shit, fella?" The bartender grinned, still smoking his opium.

"We want Shin Chi," Clint said bluntly.

"Shin Chi?" The barman smiled, revealing several gaps where teeth had once been. "I ask my friends."

He staggered toward the stevedores and held up a hand to make an announcement. The four musclemen looked up and waited tensely.

"Djyow-ming," he declared. *"Gung djee!"*

"Damn it!" Wing snapped. "He sicced 'em on us!"

The stevedores immediately rose from their seats and charged the trio. Knives flashed as the dock workers drew bowies from belt sheaths. The closest man slashed his blade at the Gunsmith who jumped back and pulled his forty-five Colt before the startled stevedore could launch another attack. The man stared at the gun, dropped his knife and raised his hands in surrender.

"That's better," Clint said with a nod.

Then he kicked the stevedore in the balls. The man doubled up in agony and Clint whacked him over the skull with the barrel of his modified Colt.

The other three stevedores attacked the two detectives. John Chang pretended to make a grab for an opponent's knife. The dockworker slashed at Chang's hands before he realized it was a distraction. The detective punted a hard sidekick to the man's kneecap, shattering the joint as if it were made of glass. The stevedore screamed and toppled to the floor while his comrades kept coming.

Sam Wing turned as if to flee from a knife-wielding opponent. Instead, he slapped both hands against a tabletop and used it for a brace as he kicked both legs backward. The bottoms of his feet crashed into the aggressor's chest, propelling the man backward into a wall. Before the stunned dockworker recovered from his surprise, Wing was upon him. The detective deftly chopped the knife out of his adversary's grasp with a side of the hand stroke and immediately slammed the point of his elbow into the man's chin. The stevedore slumped, senseless, to the floor.

The bartender bolted for the backroom as fast as his chunky body allowed. The Gunsmith was a lot faster. Clint pounced on the man's back. They both fell against the door, the bartender's face connecting hard with wood. He groaned as Clint pulled him away from the door. Blood oozed from the bartender's broken nose.

"Not your day, is it?" the Gunsmith commented before he smashed his fist into the bartender's jaw. The man crashed to the floor which was already littered with his defeated friends.

The Gunsmith caught a glimpse of the battle between John Chang and the last stevedore. The larger man executed a knife thrust at the detective's stomach. Chang nimbly sidestepped out of the path of the blade and shuffled forward to attack the stevedore from behind. He quickly rammed an elbow into the aggressor's right kidney and lashed the side of his hand across the base of the man's skull. The last stevedore fell on his belly and didn't get up.

Clint turned his attention to the door. He raised a boot and slammed it into wood next to the doorknob. The door sprang open and Clint charged into the storage room, his pistol in hand.

The place was crowded with stacks of beer kegs and crates of red-eye. The Gunsmith spotted a blanket and a bowl with a pair of chopsticks jutting from it, in a corner. This was the only evidence to suggest anyone had been living in the room.

Clint approached the blanket, scanning the room for his quarry. No sign of Shin Chi or anyone else. Then he heard feet shuffle along the wooden floor. He turned to see a stack of beer kegs weave toward him.

The Gunsmith bolted away as the barrels came tumbling down. Kegs struck the floor, bursting on impact, and beer splattered across the room. A short, skinny figure darted away from the mess and dashed out the door.

The Gunsmith galloped after and found the little man in the barroom. The fellow had run right into John Chang and Sam Wing. The detectives held him prisoner, each holding an arm in a bent-wrist lock grip.

Clint recognized the fellow's timid features highlighted by the catfish mustache. It was the same face he'd seen two nights before, staring up at him from the floor after he'd knocked the intruder down with his fist.

"You understand English, fella?" the Gunsmith asked.

The man merely gazed fearfully at Clint.

The Gunsmith pointed his revolver at the captive's face and thumbed back the hammer. "You understand this?"

"Me speak English," the little Chinese replied quickly. "No kill me. Shin Chi want talk. Talk good."

"Wonderful," Clint said dryly. "Why don't you tell my friends what happened the other night. Tell them in Chinese so you don't have trouble expressing yourself."

Shin Chi eagerly exploded into a lengthy declaration in rapid Cantonese. While the thief babbled away, Clint checked on the bartender and four stevedores. The man whose leg had been broken by Chang's kick timidly crawled to the bar. The bartender and one of the other dockworkers had also regained consciousness. The Gunsmith herded them over to the bar as well.

"Our little friend has given us a full confession," Sam Wing announced after hearing Shin Chi's story. "He claims he only got involved with the Yellow Serpent Tong because he sold stolen goods to them. Apparently, Ming Chuan had been in command of finding the girl. He decided to use Shin to help him break into your room silently, without leaving evidence of a forced entry."

"Yes! Yes!" Shin cried. "I jimmy lock. Do this good, but no kill girl. Ming Chuan do that."

"If the Tong forced him to act against his will," the Gunsmith asked, "why was he carrying a gun? They must have trusted him quite a bit to let him have a pistol."

"He said Ming Chuan gave him the gun," Chang answered. "The pistol wasn't loaded. Ming Chuan didn't want any shooting. Shin was only supposed to use the pistol to frighten you and the girl."

Shin nodded vigorously. "Yes, yes."

"How come the Tong didn't kill him afterward?" Clint inquired.

"Shin fled out the window while Ming Chuan was strangling the girl," Wing replied. "He knew more Tong were waiting in the alley so he scrambled up onto the roof. He's been running ever since."

"Why didn't he go to the police?" Clint asked.

"If you were Chinese you wouldn't ask that," Wing told him. "Shin sees authority as the Manchu rulers. Would you tell the bulls you were a thief if you figured they might chop your hand off?"

"Hell, the police aren't going to hurt him," Clint said. "He'll probably be put in protective custody somewhere outside of San Francisco until he can testify against the Tong. I'm sure the authorities will be so happy to be able to stop a Tong operation, they won't give a damn about Shin's petty larceny.''

''I think you're right, Clint,'' Sam agreed. ''Maybe the police and City Hall don't care if the Tong prey on other Chinese, but the Yellow Serpent Society plans to expand operations to include more whites. They'll do something about it this time.''

''But how are we going to get Shin to the police?'' Chang wondered. ''There isn't room in the buggy and we can't simply march him through the streets all the way to the police station.''

''How about a hansom cab?'' Clint suggested.

''You'll never find one in Chinatown,'' Wing replied. ''All we can do is get Shin to Amanda's house and hide him there while we get in touch with Kovac.''

''I don't like involving Amanda in this,'' Chang replied tensely. ''Not with the Tong after all four of us. It's too dangerous.''

''I agree,'' Clint said.

''I don't like it either,'' Wing assured them, ''but what choice do we have? The Tong are probably already watching our office. Amanda's place is the only place we can go to.''

''I still don't like it.'' The Gunsmith sighed. ''But I'm afraid you're right.''

Chapter Twenty

"Do you guys think I'm running a flophouse here?" Amanda Lincoln asked when Clint and the two detectives escorted Shin Chi into the house.

"You just have to hold him here for a couple hours," Sam Wing assured her.

"Bringing Clint here is one thing," she said, "but bringing a criminal here is quite another."

"She's right," Chang agreed. "Let me take Shin Chi to the police. The rest of you stay here."

"With the Tong after you?" Amanda glared at him. "You're not going anywhere alone."

"I can take care of myself," he insisted.

"You know the way the Tong are," she countered. "You need someone to watch your back. To take on the Tong single-handed is insane—even for a man like you, John."

"Amanda—" Chang began.

"Please, John," Amanda pleaded, taking one of Chang's hands in both of hers.

"Very well," he agreed with a thin smile.

"Okay," Wing began. "How about John and I go to the police? Clint will stay here and guard Shin."

"That sounds fine to me," the Gunsmith replied. "But it's Amanda's house."

"I guess that's the best arrangement," she agreed. "Just make sure you're careful."

"We're not taking any chances we don't have to," Wing assured her as he held up a pair of handcuffs. "Where do you want us to plant Shin until we can get the bulls to uproot him?"

"Will he be all right in the basement?" Amanda asked.

"He'll be right at home," Wing replied. "I'll cuff him to the railing at the foot of the stairs."

"Sam," Clint said, "try to impress upon him that we don't want to hurt him. We'll protect him from the Tong if he helps us. Okay?"

"Sure." Wing nodded as he grabbed Shin Chi by an elbow. "Come on, weasel breath. I'm gonna show you your new burrow."

"It shouldn't take us long to find Inspector Kovac," Chang told Clint and Amanda as he watched Wing haul Shin into the next room. "But we'd better contact him directly. The Tong may have an informer on the police force."

"Shin isn't going anywhere," Clint assured him.

"Shin doesn't worry me," the detective replied. "The Tong may be able to track us to Amanda's house. We can't be certain how much they know about— about our friendship with her. Stay alert, Clint."

"I intend to," the Gunsmith replied.

"John, don't worry." Amanda smiled. "I don't think the Yellow Serpent Society has a file on your life history."

"Especially concerning matters that ended long ago," Chang remarked. "Perhaps you're right, but I wish we'd never involved you in this business."

"Shin is safe and sound and most of all secure,"

Sam Wing announced as he strolled back into the room. "The basement is a little cleaner than what he's used to. Maybe we can pick up a couple rats for him to play with when we get back."

"Let's get going," Chang urged. "I'd like to get this over with as soon as possible."

The two detectives left. Amanda locked the door and turned to face the Gunsmith. "I suppose you wonder what that was all about," she said.

"I don't reckon it's any of my business, Amanda," he replied.

"I'm sure you've figured it out already," she stated. "After all, I did tell you I'd had a love affair with a Chinese man."

"You also said he was terrific." The Gunsmith smiled. "To be honest, I wondered if that man had been John or Sam."

"You probably would have guessed Sam, right?"

"Not after I saw you and John exchange bittersweet glances over breakfast."

"He's a very fine man," Amanda stated. "They both are. Sam seems a bit hard-boiled and carefree, but he's more sensitive than he appears to be. John on the other hand seems so very Oriental. Cool, calm, always in control. Disciplined in mind and body and totally at peace with himself."

"Pretty much so," Clint agreed.

"Unfortunately," she said, "that's exactly what he's like. He's formed an invisible wall around his emotions. In a way, you're a lot like John."

Clint grinned. "Am I terrific too?"

"You know you are." Amanda laughed. "But I don't think I could get through your wall either, Clint. A woman can't commit herself to someone unless she knows who that man really is. It's not enough to love someone and know that he loves you. A woman has to know every side of a man's personality. She has to be able to understand everything that drives him and everything he feels."

"Amanda, that's impossible. You can never hope to know *yourself* that well, let alone have such deep insight into somebody else. We all have those walls around our emotions. We have to have them. It's part of human nature to protect oneself and nothing is more vulnerable than a man's heart."

"I never wanted to hurt him," she declared. "Just as I'd never want to hurt you."

"Maybe John is afraid of hurting you," he replied. "I know I am."

"You're a wonderful man, Clint," she said as she crossed the room to the liquor cabinet. "But you'll never be able to have a permanent relationship with a woman, will you?"

"I doubt it," the Gunsmith admitted. "But then again, I'm not so sure I want one."

"Just enjoy yourself and move on then?" Amanda shook her head. "Do you think memories will be enough in your old age?"

"I don't think I'll have to worry about growing old." Clint shrugged. "Of course, I didn't think I'd live to see forty either."

"What if you're wrong this time too?"

"I'll worry about growing old when I start to feel old," the Gunsmith told her.

"You're not afraid of being alone?" Amanda asked as she poured them each a glass of brandy.

"I spend a lot of time by myself," Clint told her as he took one of the drinks.

"What do you think about when you're on the trail alone?" she asked, sipping her brandy.

"A lot of things. I look forward to the future, I try to accept the present and I make an effort to forget everything in the past that wasn't pleasant."

"Do you think you'll remember me, Clint?"

"Yes, indeed," he assured her.

"Let's make sure," Amanda remarked as she placed her drink on the coffee table.

Clint followed her example. No sooner had he put down his glass than Amanda was in his arms. She snaked her arms around his neck and pressed her mouth to his. They embraced and kissed for several minutes, savoring each other's touch.

Amanda's hand slipped between Clint's legs and massaged his erection. The Gunsmith moved his lips to the girl's neck and kissed her, moving his mouth to her ear. He gently chewed the soft lobe and ran his tongue along the mastoid.

"Amanda, this really isn't the time for it," he whispered. "I'm sorry . . ."

"You want to as badly as I do," she insisted as she began to unbutton his fly.

"We can't go to bed together when the Tong might show up at any second and we've got a prisoner in the basement," the Gunsmith rasped, unable to repress a sigh of pleasure as she freed his member and stroked it with her fingers.

"The Tong couldn't possibly know about me unless they followed you and John and Sam here," Amanda said, gently pulling his penis to and fro. "That man in the basement is handcuffed to the rail and we don't have to go to bed to make love."

"I'll have to keep my gun within arm's reach,"

Clint told her. "And we'll have to get dressed just as soon as we finish."

"Whatever you say, Clint," Amanda agreed.

The Gunsmith's common sense told him not to do it. He knew he should resist her advances, but a man can convince himself a lot of things make sense when passion dominates his senses.

"Let me check on Shin Chi first."

"I'll be waiting," Amanda promised with a smile.

Chapter Twenty-One

"You no must chain me up, Clint-sir," Shin Chi declared when the Gunsmith descended the basement stairs to check on the prisoner.

"We don't want you to get any silly notions about running off again," Clint told him as he checked the handcuffs.

"Where would I run, Clint-sir," the Chinese asked. "Tong kill me if catch."

"You're not afraid of the police?" Clint inquired, making certain the handrail was solid.

"You say police no hurt me," Shin replied. "That truth, yes? No lie Shin. Truth?"

"It's the truth, fella," Clint assured him. "But I still doubt that you're exactly looking forward to talking to the boys in blue."

"Where place call In Bloo?" Shin asked. "Why me talk to boys not to police?"

"Trust me." Clint rolled his eyes. "You'll talk to the police."

"That good." Shin nodded. "Me talk police. Talk them about Tong, yes?"

"That's right," the Gunsmith said. "I'll be back and check on you after a while. See if I can get you some water and maybe some food."

"Like food, water." Shin smiled. "Thank, Clint-sir."

The Gunsmith climbed to the head of the stairs and entered the kitchen. He moved on to the sitting room to find Amanda sprawled across a patchwork quilt on the floor. She was totally naked.

"I see you've been busy," he said.

"Just getting a few things ready for you, Clint," Amanda replied. "Now let's get busy together."

Clint quickly stripped off his clothes. He placed the New Line Colt twenty-two inside a boot before he lay down beside the girl. Then he put the gunbelt with his forty-five within easy arm's reach.

"You feel more relaxed now, darling?" Amanda asked, combing her fingers through the carpet of hair on his chest.

"I'm getting there," he assured her.

"I can tell," she grinned as she stroked him.

Amanda surprised the Gunsmith when she shifted her head to his crotch. Her warm soft lips slipped over the head of his penis, her tongue caressing the sensitive foreskin. Gradually, she slid her mouth down the length of his shaft. She raised and lowered her head, riding her lips up and down his throbbing cock.

When he was fully erect, she mounted him, rocking gently, working him deeper inside her hot woman-hood. Then she began to pump herself along his hard shaft, riding him like a pony. She hummed happily and bounced faster.

Clint had never been a selfish lover. He considered his partner's satisfaction to be as important as his own. The Gunsmith arched his back and pumped his hips to drive himself deeper into the girl.

Amanda groaned and cried out in ecstasy as the first orgasm shot through her like an electric bolt. She sat, impaled upon Clint's manhood, her head bowed as she caught her breath. Then she repeated the procedure a second time.

The Gunsmith paced himself with her movement. The girl gasped as she approached climax and Clint came just as Amanda convulsed in erotic joy, bursting into another orgasm.

"Oh, Clint," she whispered, "you really are special."

"So are you," the Gunsmith replied as he kissed her cheek. "But we have to get up."

"Already?" She pouted.

"I'm afraid so," Clint told her.

He withdrew from her and grabbed his gunbelt, keeping it close by as he pulled on his clothes.

"Are you hungry?" Amanda asked, climbing into her dress.

"Yeah," Clint replied, suddenly realizing he hadn't eaten all day. "Could you get something for Shin too?"

"Sure." Amanda shrugged. "Poor little guy is probably hungry too."

Clint checked the front door while Amanda padded barefoot into the kitchen. The Gunsmith assured himself the door was locked and securely bolted. He peered out a window. The street appeared to be deserted.

The crash of splintering wood and exploding glass came from the kitchen. Amanda screamed. The Gunsmith whirled, drawing his pistol, and dashed to the next room.

Amanda stood in the middle of the kitchen, her eyes wide with terror. A hard-faced Chinese stood beside her. He yanked her hair with one hand, pulling her head back to expose Amanda's throat to the knife he held in his other fist.

"Drop the knife!" Clint ordered, aiming his gun at the Tong killer.

"He will not," a voice with a clipped British accent announced.

The Gunsmith turned to the broken remnants of the back door. He blinked with surprise when he saw the pasty-faced figure who stepped across the threshold.

It was Mao Chu, the head of the Yellow Serpent Tong.

Chapter Twenty-Two

"He will not drop the knife," Mao Chu declared. "He will not drop it because he is loyal to me. Yuan has been a member of my Tong since birth. His father belonged to the Yellow Serpent Society and his father before him."

Mao still appeared as cool and emotionless as before. He wore a dark gray cotton suit and a matching derby. The Tong leader looked like a hard-nosed, ruthless businessman, which was exactly how he regarded himself. Two more Tong enforcers stood beside their master, their faces as hard as stone with slithers of onyx for eyes.

"That means he's willing to die for you, Mao?" Clint Adams asked. He didn't turn his attention from the man who held a knife to Amanda's throat.

"Not for me," Mao replied. "For his honor."

"What honor is there in dying for the sake of a heartless son of a bitch like you?"

"You do not understand us, Mr. Adams," Mao said. "Yuan's family has belonged to the Yellow Serpent Tong or an organization similar to it for centuries. His ancestors' noble ranks extend to the White Lotus Society which fought the Mongols long ago. It is a matter of honor to obey his leader."

"He's more afraid of losing face than losing his life?" the Gunsmith asked.

"Yuan's honor alone is not at stake," Mao explained. "To act with cowardice would be to blemish the history of his entire family. Tradition is something you Americans do not understand. How can you? Your country is a wailing infant hardly a century old. We, however, have come from a culture with thousands of years development. We know the value of honor and courage. Life is nothing compared to this."

"You speak of honor and courage," Clint scoffed. "Lofty words from a castrated bandit chief. What honor is there in selling opium? How much courage does it take to order the murder of a young woman?"

"We've already discussed this, Mr. Adams," Mao said. "I do not apologize for my business. I earn a considerable profit. You and I know it is being invested to form an invisible empire here in this country. An empire I will reign over. But these men do not understand that. Obviously they do not understand English either or I wouldn't be speaking so frankly to you this moment."

"I can guess what they think the Yellow Serpent Society is for," the Gunsmith said dryly. "They think you're saving up money to form an army to return to China and defeat the Manchu government."

"Fan Ching, fu Ming," Mao Chu declared.

The Tong enforcers seemed to swell with pride. Their eyes flashed with determination as they repeated the expression, chanting as one might recite a mystical spell.

"It means 'Overthrow the Ching Dynasty, restore the Ming Dynasty,' " Mao explained. "That is what they understand. They will indeed die to support that slogan. They feel that disobeying me will dishonor them as loyal opponents of the Manchu's Ching Dynasty. Even if you could speak Chinese, Mr. Adams, you would not be able to convince them to believe otherwise."

"I'm not going to try, Mao," the Gunsmith replied as he swung the modified Colt toward the Tong leader. He pointed the gun at Mao's chest.

"A change of tactics, Mr. Adams?" the Yellow Serpent boss smiled.

"Your men may be willing to die for the Tong's noble cause, but you know it's a lie, Mao," Clint told him. "Are you ready to give your life for that lie?"

"I too have my honor, Mr. Adams," the Tong leader said simply, apparently unafraid of Clint's pistol.

"Bullshit," the Gunsmith replied. "You don't know what honor is, Mao. You certainly don't have any family tradition to uphold, do you?"

"You are wrong, Mr. Adams," Mao said. "I do."

"Really?" Clint sneered. "Do you even know who your parents were, Mao? They sold you to the Manchu rulers to be castrated like a pig. Tell me you love and respect your ancestors, court eunuch. Tell me why you'd be willing to die for their honor."

"You misunderstand, Mr. Adams," Mao replied, a hard edge in his voice. "My family tradition is one I have started. I am not a young man. As you have said, I am incapable of having sons to carry on that tradition. The Tong is my family, Mr. Adams, and I will die to uphold its honor. What else do I have to believe in?"

"I play a lot of poker, Mao," Clint said. "I can usually tell when a man is bluffing."

"If that is what you believe," the Tong boss began,

"kill me. I will die with the satisfaction of knowing you and Miss Lincoln will die as well. Shoot me and Yuan will cut her throat. You may kill him, but Moy and Hieh will certainly take your life as well."

Mao gestured with his palms upraised. "The choice is yours, Mr. Adams. Drop your gun and come with me or pull the trigger. We can either leave here together alive or die together. It makes little difference to me either way."

"You know what, Mao?" the Gunsmith said. "I don't think you're bluffing."

He lowered his pistol and sighed in surrender.

Chapter Twenty-Three

Suddenly, faster than a man can blink, Clint Adams raised the modified Colt and opened fire. A forty-five-caliber slug smashed into Yuan's forehead. The Tong enforcer's head snapped back, brains gushing from his shattered skull. The knife fell from lifeless fingers as Yuan's body fell.

Amanda screamed in revulsion as the corpse slid against her on its way to the floor. The Gunsmith ignored her cry and immediately swung his revolver toward the three men at the door. The forty-five roared again and one of Mao's escort members hurtled into a wall with a bullet in his heart.

The other bodyguard reached inside his jacket for a weapon. He did not live to use it. The Gunsmith shot him in the face. The Tong enforcer was kicked backward by the impact of the bullet. He clamped both hands over his bullet-shattered features and fell through the doorway and tumbled outside.

"You still want to die, Mao?" Clint asked, aiming his pistol at the Tong leader.

"A very bold move, Mr. Adams," Mao said with admiration. "You gambled the lives of yourself and the girl on your skill."

"There wasn't any other choice that made sense," the Gunsmith replied.

"I could have been killed!" Amanda exclaimed, glaring at Clint.

"Calm down," the Gunsmith told her. "If I'd surrendered Mao would have ordered his man to cut your throat. What would he need you alive for? I'm the one he wants."

"You and Shin Chi," Mao declared. "We know he's here. You and those two detectives were careless when you talked about your plans in the Dragonfly Tavern. You must have forgotten the bartender understood English."

"The police will be here soon," Clint stated. "You can talk to them about this. They'll sure have some questions for you, fella."

"You're wrong, Mr. Adams," Mao sighed. "I will ask the questions."

"You seem to forget that the odds have changed," Clint told him. "I've got the best hand now. The one with a gun in it."

"But as you say in poker," Mao began. "I have an ace up my sleeve."

A blur of movement at the corner of Clint's eyes was the only warning he received before a hand swept against his forearm, knocking his gunhand toward the ceiling. Another hand pressed against the small of his spine, pushing him off balance.

The Gunsmith began to stagger forward, but suddenly his arm was violently twisted by a savage grasp and he found himself bent over, unable to move. A powerful opponent held his arm in a simple, yet effective, hold. One hand gripped Clint's wrist while the other pressed against the back of his elbow.

Clint gazed up at his opponent. A familiar stone face with a bald head stared down at him. Ming Chuan applied more pressure, forcing the Gunsmith to drop his pistol. Amanda screamed, but she was abruptly silenced by a blow to the side of her neck. Clint craned his head to see the girl sprawled on the floor with two more Tong enforcers standing over her.

"You bastards!" he snarled helplessly.

"Relax, Mr. Adams," Mao urged. "Otherwise I'll simply have to order Ming Chuan to break your arm. I'm sure you realize he can do that quite easily. Now, I suspect you carry another weapon hidden on your person. One of my men will search you. Do not resist. If you do, it will cause you nothing but pain."

A Tong soldier patted down Clint's torso and found the bellygun. He handed it to Mao who simply shrugged and tossed the pistol onto the kitchen table. The Yellow Serpent flunky continued to frisk Clint, checking his ankles, forearms and the nape of his neck for hidden weapons.

Other Tong members searched the house, darting from room to room. Clint figured there had to be at least half a dozen of them. The Yellow Serpent reinforcements had obviously entered through the front door while the Gunsmith's attention had been on Mao and his three bodyguards. Clint cursed himself for his carelessness, but he didn't dwell on it. There wasn't time to bemoan mistakes. He had to come up with a plan of how to escape—which, at the moment, seemed impossible.

"Have you ever heard of Sun Tzu, Mr. Adams?" Mao inquired. "He wrote the *Ping Fa*, the first textbook on the principles of war and espionage, five hundred years before the birth of Christ, as you Americans like to say when referring to an incident in history. Among other things, it teaches that a commander never attacks from only one position and how to make the most of distractions in combat.''

"I'd sure like to read that book," Clint remarked. "If you'll let me borrow it, I promise to give it back to you next week."

"You really are amusing, Mr. Adams. Now, where is Shin Chi?''

"Beats the hell out of me," Clint replied.

"We'll do worse than that if you don't answer my question," Mao warned.

Clint saw two Tong enforcers emerge from the basement. He held his breath, waiting for the pair to report their discovery to Mao Chu. To his astonishment, the men simply shook their heads.

"I'll ask you again, Mr. Adams," Mao began, "where is Shin Chi?''

"You checked up your ass for him yet?" Clint answered.

"You'll regret your insolence, Mr. Adams," Mao promised.

He barked a series of rapid orders to his men. Two Tong enforcers gathered up Amanda Lincoln's unconscious body and carried her outside. Clint struggled against Ming Chuan's arm-lock, but soon realized the effort would only earn him a disabled limb.

"Where are you taking her?" the Gunsmith demanded.

"Do not worry," Mao told him. "You're coming with us as well. The police may arrive here soon. Even if your detective friends haven't gone to fetch them, the gunshots may attract the attention of the local constable. We'll simply have to take you somewhere else to receive a proper interrogation performed by a true expert at wrenching information from stubborn victims.''

The Gunsmith's stomach knotted with fear as he recalled Mao's tale about the Death of a Thousand Cuts.

"I told you you would regret your insolence, Mr. Adams." Mao smiled cruelly.

Chapter Twenty-Four

The Gunsmith was escorted to a large, box-shaped delivery wagon parked on the curb in front of Amanda's house. Four Tong enforcers escorted him to the vehicle. Only one man had a pistol, but two others held fighting hatchets in their fists. The fourth was Ming Chūan, armed only with his deadly hands; he didn't need any other weapon. Clint realized he wouldn't have a prayer against the huge *wu-shu* expert.

They climbed into the back of the wagon. Amanda was already inside. She moaned as consciousness returned. The girl began to sit up, rubbing the side of her neck, wincing with pain. The Gunsmith sat on the floor beside her.

"You okay?" he asked.

"I think so," she replied, shaking her head to clear it. "John once told me something about a blow to the neck muscle being one of the best ways to render a person unconscious with the least chance of causing any serious injury."

"You'll be sore for a couple hours and then you'll hardly notice it," Clint told her. "I got hit the same way in my hotel room a couple of nights ago. That bald-headed ape over there was the one who did the honors."

Ming Chuan, with his legs crossed in a half lotus position, sat facing the couple. The big Chinese folded his arms on his chest and watched the pair like a snake waiting for a rabbit to venture out of its hole. The other three Tong members also sat within the wagon. Clint clenched his teeth in helpless rage. Unarmed, there was no way he could take on his captors. Ming Chuan alone would be more than he could handle without a weapon.

"Where's Shin Chi?" Amanda asked in a soft whisper. "Did they find him?"

"No," Clint replied. "And they looked in the basement. My guess is the little sneak picked the lock to his handcuffs. Shin's an expert at breaking and entry. We should have figured those cuffs wouldn't hold him."

"There's a coal bin in the basement," Amanda told Clint. "It has a chute that leads outside. Shin must have found it and escaped."

"If he heard the Tong upstairs and the shooting," the Gunsmith said, "you can bet he ran out of the area faster than a jackrabbit with a coyote at its heels. He's probably halfway to the Nevada border by now."

"Where are they taking us?" Amanda asked.

"I don't know," Clint replied. "But it's probably going to be a pretty unpleasant experience."

"There has to be some way out of this mess," she said fearfully.

"We're still alive," Clint reminded her. "That means there's still hope. Maybe the Tong will get careless and we'll have a better chance to escape."

"What if that doesn't happen?"

"I'm too busy praying it will."

"Be serious, Clint."

"Okay," the Gunsmith whispered. "It can't hurt to tell them that we had Shin in the basement. Maybe they'll even send somebody to check the house again and John and Sam and the police will catch the guy and wring some information out of him. If they ask about John and Sam, tell them our friends went back to the detective office. I'm sure they have enough sense not to go back there without the police for backup."

"I don't want to sound selfish," Amanda began, "but what about us?"

"We'll just have to do the best we can and try to keep our heads."

"They're going to torture us, aren't they?" she asked fearfully.

"We don't know that."

"Then why didn't they just kill us?" Amanda asked.

"They might want to hold us and use us for bait to try to lure John and Sam into a trap."

"You don't really believe that . . ."

"I believe we can't afford to panic," Clint insisted. "All we can do is stay alert and pray something will happen that we can take advantage of."

They could only guess how long they rode in the enclosed back of the delivery wagon until they finally came to a halt. Tension and fear exaggerate time. A second can seem like an hour, a minute can be a lifetime. Clint wasn't certain if they rode in the wagon for half an hour or half a year.

At last the wagon stopped. Ming Chuan and the other Tong goons opened the back door and gestured at Clint and Amanda.

"*Chu lai!*" Ming Chuan snapped. "*Chu lai!*"

"I think that means our presence is requested outside," the Gunsmith said dryly. "You gonna be okay, Amanda?"

"That depends on what they do to us," she replied. "But I don't think we'll make things any better by getting these guys pissed off enough to climb in here after us."

"Hold a second," Clint rasped when he noticed the butt of a pistol jutting from the belt of one of the Tong who stood at the opening. "You get out first. Pretend to stumble and twist your ankle."

"*Chu lai!*" Ming Chuan ordered angrily.

"We're coming, pal," Clint assured him. "Amanda?"

"Okay," she said reluctantly.

The girl climbed out of the wagon. She appeared to slip and tumbled to the ground with a cry of pain. The Tong enforcers turned toward her for a split second—long enough for the Gunsmith to make his move.

He lashed a foot into the face of the closest Tong thug. He was grateful it wasn't Ming Chuan, who he suspected would have caught his leg and yanked it out of the socket. His boot crashed into the man's mouth, shattering teeth and bone.

The Tong hoodlum fell to the ground. Clint leaped into his prime target, the pistol-packing Chinese. The man yelped in surprise as Clint landed on him. Both men tumbled to the ground. Clint punched the man in the mouth and hammered the bottom of his fist into the Tong's face. Blood squirted from his nostrils when his nose broke.

The Gunsmith yanked the pistol from his opponent's belt and pivoted on one knee to confront Ming Chuan and the remaining Tong enforcer. He suddenly realized

Ming Chuan had already closed in. The big Chinese grabbed Clint's fist around the gun butt, his fingers pinning Clint's thumb to prevent him from cocking the single-action revolver.

Clint desperately tried to hook his left fist into Ming Chuan's groin. The *wu-shu* expert moved a bent knee in front of his crotch. Clint's knuckles cracked painfully against the hard bony joint.

The Gunsmith leaped to his feet and tried to throw a punch at Ming Chuan's face and simultaneously stomp a boot heel into the big man's instep. Clint's foot only stamped the ground and his fist was parried by the back of Ming Chuan's right hand. The Tong killer's left hand remained clamped around the Gunsmith's thumb and the pistol.

Ming Chuan quickly stabbed the tips of his stiff fingers into Clint's solar plexus. The Gunsmith's breath exploded from his lungs from the nerve-scorching blow. It felt as if Ming Chuan had shoved a knife blade into his chest.

Winded and semiparalyzed, the Gunsmith was too dazed to react as Ming Chuan wrenched the gun from his hand. The Chinese brute tossed the pistol aside and promptly slashed the side of his left hand into Clint's bread basket. The Gunsmith groaned and doubled up. He fell to his knees, nearly choking as bile rose to his throat.

Clint glanced up through blurry eyes to see Ming Chuan towering over him, a cold smile on his merciless, hard face. The Chinese held his hands out, palms up, fingers wiggling to invite the Gunsmith to get up and try again. Clint spat a glob of vomit and raised his hands in surrender before he rose to his feet.

"Mr. Adams," Mao Chu said wearily, "what is the

meaning of this nonsense?''

"Ming Chuan and I were just showing each other a few fighting tricks," Clint replied. "Tell him he did okay. We'll call this round a draw."

Amanda stood between two Tong enforcers. Each held one of her arms. She looked at Clint sadly and shrugged. The Gunsmith responded with the same gesture.

"Come along, Mr. Adams," Mao ordered. "You're beginning to annoy me."

"Heaven forbid," the Gunsmith muttered.

Chapter Twenty-Five

It was then the Gunsmith saw where they were. The wagon was parked on a cobblestone driveway extending from an iron-framed gate to to a large white stone mansion. The house was a strange combination of architectural styles. White pillars supported the porch roof; balconies with spandrel-shaped windows were an odd cross of French and Islamic styles. The rooftops, however, featured the long graceful sloping design of a pagoda.

"Are we supposed to guess what it is?" the Gunsmith asked.

"It is my home," Mao Chu declared.

"You have my sympathies," Clint told him.

"I'm becoming very tired of your insulting remarks, Mr. Adams," the Tong leader warned. "If you open your mouth again it had better be to answer a question. Is that understood?"

"I'm allowed to say yes, right?" the Gunsmith inquired.

"Come along, Mr. Adams," Mao commanded.

Escorted by the Tong enforcers, Clint and Amanda were marched up the front steps. The door opened and a Chinese clad in white bowed respectfully to Mao Chu. The Tong boss led the way inside.

They entered a stunning hallway with gleaming white walls. Large Oriental vases and Asian ferns in decorative pots added color to the room.

Mao led them into a far more splendid room. French furniture and a multicolored Afghan carpet were a sharp contrast to the collection of jade and ivory. Most appeared to be statues of elderly Chinese men dressed in fancy robes and circular caps. Mao noticed Clint gazing at the figures with interest.

"The collection consists of some of the greatest leaders in China's history," Mao explained. "They've all been a great inspiration to the Yellow Serpent Tong. You'll find Confucius, Sun Tzu, Emperor Wu and Kwan Ti, the god of war, here."

"Bet most of those fellas would just as soon not be here," the Gunsmith muttered under his breath.

"What was that, Mr. Adams?" Mao demanded.

"Nothing you'd care to hear," the Gunsmith replied.

"Then I won't ask you to repeat it," the Tong leader said briskly.

He continued to lead them through the great house. The next room was a large gymnasium. Rows of Chinese weapons were mounted on racks by the walls. Clint gazed over the assortment of swords, spears, knives and fighting staves. A few weapons were totally alien to him. There were three section sticks attached by chain links and an object that resembled a thick length of bamboo mounted on a haft like a sword complete with a full quillion.

"This is where your men practice *wu-shu*?" the Gunsmith asked.

"Yes," Mao replied. "They train with bare hands and with the traditional weapons of China. The double-edged sword is called a *chien*, the broad-bladed 'butterfly knives' are called *tao*, the three-section staff is a *san-chieh-kan*, the wooden whip you were looking at is a *tieh pien* and the fighting hatchet—the traditional weapon of the Tong—is called a *fu*.''

"Are we going to be quizzed on Chinese terms later?" Clint asked dryly.

"Sorry if I bored you, Mr. Adams." Mao smiled. "Believe me, you'll soon be begging for a little boredom.''

"I was afraid you'd say something like that," the Gunsmith remarked.

"You don't know what fear is," the Tong leader told him. *"Not yet."*

"Wanna bet?" Clint muttered.

The next room was a large dining hall which contained several long tables with benches. Nine Tong enforcers, dressed in blue pajamalike jackets and trousers, were eating fish and rice with chopsticks. The men immediately rose and bowed as Mao entered the room. Clint wondered how many other Tong were lurking in the mansion

As far as he could tell there were at least fifteen Tong soldiers in the house and probably more. Even if Clint could get his hands on a gun, the odds would be overwhelmingly in favor of the enemy. Fighting them with his fists would be suicide. Every one of them was better trained in hand to hand than the Gunsmith.

Mao addressed the men in the dining hall in Cantonese, but Clint noticed the Tong leader pointed at Amanda Lincoln and then spread his hands when he faced the enforcers. The Chinese grinned happily and rose from their seats. They rushed forward and seized Amanda. She screamed as the men pulled her toward the exit.

She tried to fight them, slashing clawed fingers at

their eyes and kicking furiously. There were too many of them. The Chinese soon grabbed all four of her limbs. Amanda's body was carried from the room, her skirt bunched up to her waist by eager, probing fingers.

"No!" the Gunsmith shouted as he charged after the gang.

Ming Chuan stepped into his path and quickly punted the heel of his palm into Clint's breastbone. The blow knocked Clint off balance. He staggered backward, nearly falling. Two lesser Tong enforcers grabbed his arms and twisted them behind his back.

"Damn you, Mao!" the Gunsmith snarled at the Yellow Serpent leader. "They'll tear her apart like a pack of rabid wolves!"

"Indeed," Mao replied calmly. "The girl has to die anyway. Why shouldn't my men enjoy her for entertainment? I must think of the morale of my troops. Another lesson from the *Ping Fa*, Mr. Adams."

"You ball-less son of a bitch," Clint spat. "Isn't there anything human inside you? Isn't there any feeling left that isn't warped and demented by bitterness and hate?"

"That depends on one's point of view, Mr. Adams."

"How the hell can you stand to live with yourself?" the Gunsmith snarled.

"Since childhood I've known the true nature of man," Mao told Clint. "My parents sold me so they could receive a few shillings for a son who would otherwise have been an extra mouth to feed. The Manchu royalty gelded me as one might livestock. They made me clean their floors and dump their buckets of piss and fed me their table scraps as if I was a dog."

"Amanda isn't a Manchu emperor," Clint insisted.

"Everybody in the world isn't planning to hurt you or try to rob you of dignity or your manhood."

"Manhood?" Mao laughed. "Don't you remember? That was removed with a knife long ago."

"Having a pair of testicles doesn't make you a man," Clint told him. "Responsibility for your own actions does."

"Really?" Mao raised his eyebrows. "Perhaps you'd like to find out what it's like to be a eunuch, Mr. Adams. I wonder how much of your compassion and humanity would remain after you'd been castrated."

"I wouldn't lash out at innocent people who never meant me any harm," Clint replied. "For the love of God . . ."

"God?" Mao said savagely. "Yes, tell me about your Christian god, Mr. Adams. I've met some of your men of god. Didn't you wonder where I learned to speak English? I learned from the Jesuit priests."

Mao clenched his fists with rage. "You see, the noble British have a good deal of influence in China. In fact, they encourage the opium trade because it helps to keep the wogs, as they call us, under control. You doubt that, Mr. Adams? The Taiping Rebellion was a protest against the opium business. Who crushed it? The British. They even burned down several Imperial palaces in 1860 when certain members of the Manchu government tried to reduce the amount of opium being grown and sold in China.

"Obviously," Mao continued, "communication with the British was important. Since I was a bright lad and already chosen to be a court eunuch, I was sent to the Jesuits to be taught English. They were Portuguese, but two of them had been educated in England. They gave me lessons in English, Latin and their accursed religion. They also beat me and flogged me just as the Manchu tyrants did. Beat the devil out of the little heathen, don't you know.''

He slowly raised a hand to the right side of his face. ''And when I refused to accept their Christian god or indeed believe any religion—for what just god worthy of worship would permit the atrocities that take place every day in this world?''—Mao hooked his fingers inside his own eyelid—''they demonstrated a parable of their gentle Lord Jesus. Matthew five, verse twenty-nine: *If thy right eye offend thee*. . .' ''

Mao ripped his hand away from his face and held out his fist.

'' *Pluck it out*,' '' he concluded as he opened his hand.

The Gunsmith gazed down at the glass eye in the center of Mao's palm.

''Oh, my God,'' Clint Adams whispered.

''You still believe in such a being?'' Mao asked, staring at Clint with his single left eye. The lids had collapsed around the empty socket of his right like a pair of empty sacks.

''God didn't do that to you,'' Clint told him. ''Fanatics who twisted Scripture—''

''Man's nature is brutal,'' Mao snapped. ''Chinese, Manchu, Portuguese, British, American—all are the same. So that girl will be raped repeatedly and her throat cut when it's finished. I've experienced far worse. I have no sympathy for her or for you, Mr. Adams.''

Mao returned the glass eye to its socket. He made certain the lids were securely draped over the artificial orb before he spoke again.

''And I assure you,'' he told the Gunsmith. ''You

will suffer far more than she unless you decide to cooperate.''

He's insane, the Gunsmith thought. *But who can blame him? Mao Chu has been through enough to drive ten men crazy.*

Clint wondered what ordeal the madman had in store for him. If he survived, would the Gunsmith be sane when it was over?

''We've wasted enough time,'' Mao declared. ''Come with me, Mr. Adams.''

Chapter Twenty-Six

It was the product of the darkest side of man's nature, a creation of the worst nightmares imaginable. Clint Adams felt a cold scorpion of ice crawl up his spine as he glanced around the room.

Shackles for wrists and ankles were mounted on the walls and dangled from chains in the ceiling. Instruments of torture were laid out on a white silk mat on a tabletop. Long metal needles, thin bladed knives similar to a doctor's scalpel, iron pliers and sticks with steel hooks attached were displayed as one might precious gems.

The Gunsmith felt his stomach knot as he speculated on the purpose for each instrument. He immediately realized this would only make the ordeal worse. Clint had never had the grisly fascination with torture needed to make a study of it, but he knew that mental torment is as much a part of such ghastly business as physical pain.

Clint turned his head away from the torture tools only to face more insidious devices. A metal dish mounted on a tripod stood at the wall and a pair of bamboo poles propped against a corner.

"Getting nervous, Mr. Adams?" Mao Chu asked.

The Tong leader, Ming Chuan and another pair of Chinese thugs had escorted the Gunsmith to the basement level. They passed through a number of cells with barred doors. The torture chamber was located at the end of the corridor.

"If you plan to rent this room," Clint said, trying to sound calmer than he felt, "you'd better change the décor."

"You won't be so cocky in a few minutes, Mr. Adams," Mao assured him.

A short fat Oriental appeared at the doorway. His round face was highlighted by a flabby double chin which made him resemble an overweight toad. The fat man bowed to his Tong master. His tiny pig eyes turned to Clint Adams and an oily smile slithered across his thick lips.

"Ah," the gross Oriental declared, "we have white man. I like work on white man. Never have white before. Always want, but never until now have white man."

"This is Mr. Clint Adams," Mao said, as if the Gunsmith were a guest at a tea party. "Mr. Adams, meet Po Qua Tu. Mr. Po is a professional torturer."

"Hello, Mr. Adams." Po smiled and bowed at Clint.

"You should both be honored," Mao explained. "Mr. Adams is a famous man known as the Gunsmith. Mr. Po is the only full-time professional torturer in San Francisco. The Yellow Serpent Society is the only Tong in the entire United States which has a resident torturer."

"Sshh," Clint said. "Not so loud or everybody will want one."

"He make joke." Po chuckled. "Me like funny man. He make me laugh plenty. He not laugh much when me work on him, but I laugh plenty."

"It's torture just listening to this guy," the Gunsmith muttered.

"All right, Mr. Po," Mao began. "We want Mr. Adams to tell us a few things . . ."

"Wait a minute," the Gunsmith interrupted. "You and I both know I'm going to talk if he starts whittling on me. What's the point in going through all that trouble?"

"No trouble." Po grinned. "Me want work on you, funny man."

"That'd be trouble for me, fella," Clint said.

"Then you're willing to answer some questions?" Mao asked. "You'll tell me where I can find Shin Chi and the two detectives? You'll tell me how much you've learned about my organization and whether you've relayed any of this information to the police?"

"I'll answer all of those questions," the Gunsmith answered. "But first you have to let the girl go. Get her away from those bastards and take her home. Then I'll talk."

"Mr. Adams"—Mao shook his head—"let's not insult each other's intelligence. You must realize I can't allow you or the young lady to leave here alive. All I can promise is a quick and relatively painless death."

"That's a lousy deal," the Gunsmith said dryly.

"Would you rather be tortured to death?" The Tong leader shrugged.

"That's some choice," the Gunsmith replied. "Okay. I'll talk. Shin Chi was in the basement. He must have escaped when you and your boys broke into Amanda's house. John Chang and Sam Wing are hiding in their office—"

"Why would they choose such an obvious place?"

Mao snapped. "You're lying, Mr. Adams."

"They figure it's so obvious you wouldn't bother to look there," Clint lied. "Got the idea from an American wiseman named Edgar Allan Poe."

"What about my operations?" Mao demanded. "What have you told the police?"

"I haven't been able to tell them anything," Clint answered. "I'm a wanted man. Remember?"

"What about the detectives?"

"I didn't trust them enough to tell them any details." Clint lied once more. "After all, they're a couple mercenaries. How could I be sure they wouldn't turn me over to you guys in the hopes of getting a reward?"

"I don't know whether to believe you or not, Mr. Adams," the Tong leader admitted.

That was the reply Clint had hoped he'd get. He'd given Mao enough truth to make the story plausible, yet still left some room for doubt. It had been a gamble. If the Tong boss believed him, the Gunsmith may have been executed on the spot, but at least he wouldn't betray Wing and Chang. If Mao didn't believe him, Clint would probably be tortured. However, since there was now a kernel of doubt, the Gunsmith played his ace.

"If you don't believe me," he began, "why don't you have your men check the detectives' office?"

"No need for that." Mao smiled coldly. "Mr. Po will find out whether you speak the truth or not."

"Oh, shit," the Gunsmith whispered.

"Me happy get work on you," Po declared.

"I bet you are," the Gunsmith said as he charged toward the torturer.

He lashed a fist into the startled man's face and seized the dazed torturer. Clint spun Po around and shoved him toward Ming Chuan who had immediately moved in. The big *wu-shu* artist collided with Po. Ming Chuan snarled angrily and pushed the fat man aside.

Clint knew he didn't have much time to make his move. He knew he couldn't escape, but maybe he could buy a few more minutes if he could get a choke hold around Mao Chu's scrawny neck. Would the Tong back down if they thought he'd break their leader's neck?

Only one way to find out, Clint thought.

Then his plan went sour. The two lesser Tong enforcers moved between the Gunsmith and Mao. The pair pulled *fu* hatchets from their belts and held the weapons ready for combat. Clint didn't oblige them. He bolted out the door.

He literally ran into two young Chinese who were about to enter the torture chamber.

All three men were equally surprised, but the Gunsmith was the most desperate. He rammed a knee between one man's legs; the man groaned and folded up in gasping agony. Clint turned on the other Oriental, slugging a wild right cross to the Tong member's left ear. The second man fell to the floor as Clint prepared to dash down the corridor.

A powerful blow between the Gunsmith's shoulder blades propelled him face-first into a wall. Clint's forehead struck the hard surface. Bright lights seemed to pop inside his skull like firecrackers.

Strong hands seized the Gunsmith's right arm and twisted it behind his back. Clint was certain Ming Chuan had caught him. Struggling against the brute seemed pointless to the dazed and winded Gunsmith. Before Clint could decide whether to resist or not, Ming Chuan dragged him back inside the torture chamber.

"Welcome back, Mr. Adams," Mao announced. "You didn't get very far, now did you?"

"How'd you expect me to react when you tell me this guy's going to torture me?" Clint replied, jerking his head toward Po.

"Mr. Po won't conduct the interrogation alone." The Tong leader smiled. "Those two young men you knocked down happen to be his assistants."

"Aw . . . hell," the Gunsmith groaned.

"We happy get work on you," Po hissed as he wiped blood from a split lip and stared at the red stain on the back of his hand. "Much happy."

"You certainly have a way of making things more difficut for yourself, Mr. Adams." Mao sighed.

"Reckon everybody's good at something," Clint replied hopelessly.

Chapter Twenty-Seven

"Are you comfortable, Mr. Adams?" Mao Chu asked.

The Gunsmith lay on his back on the stone floor. His wrists were manacled to chains mounted to the wall and his legs were shackled to a similar set of chains which extended from the ceiling. Clint's rump and lower limbs were raised above the floor by the leg irons.

"I would have been satisfied with a chair," the Gunsmith assured him.

"Mr. Po likes to start working on a subject's feet," Mao explained. "I understand a man's feet have dozens of little bones that can be broken and nerve endings that are connected to virtually every other part of your body. Mr. Po tells me he can cause considerable pain and prolong it for hours by torturing a man's bare feet."

Po's two assistants grinned as they pulled off Clint's boots and then stripped off his socks. One of the Chinese drew a dagger from its belt sheath and grabbed Clint's big toe.

"*Bu hau!*" Po snapped. "Not yet."

The torturer approached the Gunsmith with a bamboo pole in his fists. Po raised the stave and swung it into the soles of Clint's feet. Wood slapped against flesh. The blow smarted more than Clint would have guessed, but it was hardly torment. Maybe Po wasn't all he was cracked up to be.

Then Po whacked the pole into Clint's feet twice more. The second blow made the Gunsmith wince. The third sent jets of sharp pain through the nerves of his legs.

"You see, Mr. Adams?" Mao remarked. "Torture is an art. Mr. Po is a master without equal. He'll spend hours striking your naked feet again and again. He and his assistants will take turns to prevent from getting weary of the task. Eventually your feet will blister and swell. The skin and nerves will become more sensitive to pain. You might pass out, but you won't die or go into a coma from this sort of torture. Clever, isn't it?"

"Any man who'd beat another man's feet ain't got no soul," the Gunsmith replied.

"Funny man still joke," Po said coldly. "Not joke much more. Start scream instead, yes?"

"Of course," Mao went on, "eventually your feet will be reduced to pulp. All the nerve endings will be destroyed. When that happens. Mr. Po will continue to torture other parts of your body. He might skin you alive or heat irons in his burner to scorch your flesh."

Po whacked the pole into Clint's feet again. The Gunsmith hissed through clenched teeth, but he managed to repress a cry of pain.

"We Chinese have certain traditional tortures of course," Mao declared. "I told you about the Death of a Thousand Cuts. We won't use it on you, but we may have bamboo driven under your fingernails or insert needles through flesh and muscle to scrape your bones to the marrow."

"Part of your proud heritage?" the Gunsmith sneered.

Po smashed the bamboo into the soles of Clint's feet again. This time Clint groaned as the pain branched out to his inner thighs and groin.

"I'm a bit tired, Mr. Adams, and not a young man anymore," Mao stated. "I'm going to get some rest now."

"Sorry if I kept you up past bedtime," the Gunsmith muttered.

"I'll be back to talk to you after Po has softened you up a bit." Mao turned to the torturer. "Make certain you don't kill him."

"Me be careful," Po promised.

"And don't castrate him until I return," Mao said sternly.

The Tong leader, Ming Chuan and two of the other Chinese hoodlums left the room. Po and his assistants smiled. They didn't like anyone interrupting their work.

"I hope Mao decides to go on vacation," Clint remarked.

Po slammed the pole across the soles of Clint's feet again. The Gunsmith yelped in pain as needles seemed to lance through his entire lower body. He felt his testicles shrivel and recede into his scrotum.

"No more jokes, funny man?" Po asked with a grin as he swung the stave again.

Clint tried to pull his feet away, but the bamboo still struck its intended target. The Gunsmith gasped and cursed helplessly. He strained against the shackles that held his wrists, but the manacles held fast.

"No like pain, funny man?" Po chuckled.

"No like fat pig with stick," Clint replied.

The bamboo slapped into skin once more. The Gunsmith managed to force a smile and conceal the effects of the agony that sliced through his body. Po looked down at Clint and frowned, uncertain if he had numbed the Gunsmith's nerves.

One of the torturer's assistants said something in Cantonese. Po shrugged. The other young Chinese moved to the instruments on the table and pointed at the horrible tools. He made a suggestion which seemed to please Po.

"Jesus," Clint rasped when he saw the junior torturer pick up a trio of steel needles. The other assistant hurried to the coal burner at the opposite side of the room.

"We give new pain," Po told Clint as he shuffled closer. "You hurt plenty. Make me laugh."

"You shouldn't give up on the stick so soon, Po," the Gunsmith replied.

"No tell me how do work!" the torturer complained, genuinely insulted by a victim giving him advice.

"Sorry," Clint said. "I don't know the rules to this sort of thing. It's my first time. . . ."

Po kicked Clint in the ribs. The Gunsmith grunted from the unexpected sharp pain. The torturer smiled, pleased that his subject was still capable of feeling agony.

"We scrape bones now," Po announced as he kicked Clint again.

"Why don't you unchain me and we can take turns?" the Gunsmith sneered.

Po turned his head and grinned as he watched his men light a fire in the metal tray. The tips of the needles were placed among the glowing coals.

"You hurt plenty," Po declared. "You beg me stop pain."

"Shut up and get on with it," Clint told him. "I'd rather listen to myself scream than to you gloat, so do your damnedest, you son of a bitch."

Po snapped an order in Cantonese and the two younger torturers held up the needles. The tips glowed bright orange. The evil assistants approached Clint.

The Gunsmith swallowed hard and tried to steel himself for an agonizing journey into Hell.

Chapter Twenty-Eight

Clint heard an object slice through the air. He caught a glimpse of a blurred shape hurtle toward the young torture assistants. Something hit flesh hard. The ugly crunch of bone accompanied the liquid gurgle of blood gushing from a fresh wound.

One of the young Chinese fell backward into a wall. He slid to the floor with a *fu* hatchet lodged in his forehead. The man's lifeless eyes stared at the blade buried in his skull.

"*Djyow-ming!*" Po and his surviving assistant cried in unison.

"We'll help you," a familiar voice declared. "Just like we helped your buddy."

To the Gunsmith's astonishment, John Chang and Sam Wing charged into the torture chamber. Po recoiled in terror, holding the bamboo pole in his fists. The younger torment expert lunged forward, wielding a needle in each fist.

John Chang met the Tong killer's charge while Sam Wing attacked Po. Chang's leg snapped out. His foot struck the torturer in the left wrist. Bone cracked and a needle fell from useless fingers. The Tong follower thrust his other needle at Chang's throat. The detective slammed the heel of a palm into the man's attacking arm to redirect the lunge. Then Chang grabbed the Tong member's wrist with both hands and shoved hard.

The Chinese hoodlum shrieked and staggered away from John Chang. The detective had driven the man's own weapon into his face. The needle jutted from the torturer's right eyeball. The sharp point had passed through the eyesocket to pierce the man's brain. His corpse wilted to the floor. Chang knelt beside the dead man and frisked him.

"I found a key," the detective announced. "I hope it will unlock those manacles."

"Yeah," Clint remarked, "so do I."

He glanced over at Sam Wing who had easily taken the bamboo pole away from Po. The hard-nosed detective then pinned the fat torturer to the floor and shoved the wooden shaft against Po's throat. The Tong tormentor struggled feebly until his windpipe collapsed under the bamboo instrument he had formerly used to inflict suffering on his victims.

"How'd you guys know I was here?" the Gunsmith asked as John Chang inserted the key into one of the manacles binding Clint's ankles.

"Shin Chi told us you and Amanda had been abducted by the Yellow Serpent Society," Chang explained as he turned the key. The manacle snapped open.

"Shin Chi?" Clint said with surprise. "I figured he'd be trying to get out of the state of California after he escaped from the basement of Amanda's house."

"He didn't," Sam Wing stated. "Shin was waiting for us when we returned with Inspector Kovac and a paddy wagon full of bulls. Shin told us what happened. He claimed Mao Chu himself was there."

"That's right," the Gunsmith confirmed. "Mao's a son of a bitch, but he's no coward."

"Kovac figured Mao took you to the Flowers of Paradise," Wing continued. "We tried to tell him Mao wouldn't head back to the brothel after last night's incident. John and I knew he'd bring you here, to his mansion on Knob Hill. After all, this isn't just his home. It's also the headquarters of the Yellow Serpent Society."

"How'd you get in here?" the Gunsmith asked as Chang unlocked the last manacle, freeing Clint.

"It was not difficult," John answered. "We simply climbed over the fence. There were two sentries outside the house. Sam and I overpowered them and entered through the back door."

"We've heard stories about prison cells and torture chambers in the place," Wing added. "It figured they'd have such a section in the basement level. So we found a stairwell leading down here."

"Thank God you did," Clint stated as he rose from the floor. He winced as he stood on his battered feet.

"Can you walk?" Chang asked. "Your feet appear quite swollen."

"I'll manage," the Gunsmith replied. "Where the hell are my boots?"

"I'll get them," Wing announced. "But your blistered feet would probably be better off without them."

"I'll worry about my feet," Clint told him. "Under the circumstances, that's not very important."

"Where's Amanda?" John Chang asked sternly. "What have they done to her?"

"They took her upstairs," Clint answered. "The first thing we have to do is see to her safety."

"Here are your boots." Wing handed the Gunsmith

his footgear. "And something else I think you'll be glad to have."

The detective handed Clint a revolver butt-first. The Gunsmith took the gun and smiled. It was his own forty-five-caliber double-action Colt. Clint slipped back the loading gate and turned the cylinder.

"I loaded it," Wing assured him. "Five rounds with the hammer resting on an empty chamber. The Tong were careless enough to leave the pistol and your gunbelt behind when they grabbed you at Amanda's place."

"Bring any spare ammunition?" the Gunsmith asked.

"Five more shells," Wing answered, fishing the forty-five cartridges from a pocket. "I didn't want to carry too much stuff with me. Figured I might have to move pretty fast tonight and I have my gun as well."

"Any idea how many Tong are crawling around this place?" Chang asked.

"I've seen about twenty," Clint replied. "But there could be twice as many of Mao's men here."

"Well," Wing remarked, "that's enough, isn't it?"

"Yeah." The Gunsmith nodded. "Let's go surround 'em."

Chapter Twenty-Nine

Clint Adams and the detectives emerged from the torture chamber. They moved through the corridor toward the stairs. A lone Tong enforcer appeared at the head of the stairs, casually descending the steps. John Chang immediately charged up the stairs to confront the man.

The startled Tong reached for the *fu* hatchet in his belt and swung a roundhouse kick at Chang's head. The detective's hands flashed. He deftly snared the man's leg and pulled the hoodlum off balance. The hapless Tong member plunged headfirst down the stairs. He tumbled to the bottom and lay in a dazed, bruised heap. Sam Wing stamped the edge of his foot into the man's throat to be certain he'd never get up.

"We'd better try not to do any shooting unless we have to," Sam remarked, bending over to relieve the dead man of his hatchet. "At least until we've whittled down the odds."

"That's a lot of whittling," Clint commented.

"Yeah," the detective agreed. "But we've already made a good start."

The trio mounted the stairs and moved to the dining hall. There were only two Tong enforcers in the room. They sat together, chatting in Cantonese as they ate

161

rice and sipped tea. The Gunsmith and Sam Wing marched into the dining hall to face the unprepared Tong thugs. Clint aimed his pistol at the pair, but he let the detective do the talking.

'Tau-shyang ni-mun!'' Wing ordered, holding his short-barreled S&W in one hand and the *fu* hand-axe in the other.

The Tong enforcers didn't intend to surrender. One man bolted upright and reached for a weapon in his belt while the other scrambled from his seat to dash for the next room, shouting a warning to anyone close enough to hear him.

The man's effort to alert his comrades to danger was abruptly terminated when Sam Wing hurled his hatchet at the retreating figure. The heavy blade hit the Tong trooper between the shoulder blades, breaking his spine in two. The man fell on his belly, the hatchet protruding from his back.

His partner managed to draw his own *fu* before John Chang attacked him from the rear. The detective quickly snaked one arm around the man's throat and jammed the other against the base of his opponent's skull. Chang then rammed a knee into the fellow's kidney and pulled him off balance. Vertebrae crunched as the Tong goon's neck broke.

"Next room is a training gym for *wu-shu*," Clint Adams told his friends.

"A *kwoon?*" Chang inquired.

"I guess so," the Gunsmith replied. "After that we'll come to a fancy sitting room and the main hall. That leads to the stairs."

"That's where they're holding Amanda," Chang said grimly before he marched to the next room.

"Jesus," Clint muttered. "I'm glad he's on our side."

"I bet the Tong won't be," Sam Wing remarked.

The Gunsmith, Wing and Chang entered the *kwoon* to discover half a dozen Tong flunkies had already dashed into the room and armed themselves with a variety of weapons. The Chinese criminals had obviously been attracted by their comrade's cry for help. Clint was relieved to see the enemy armed with spears, swords and hatchets. It meant they probably didn't have guns.

A spear-wielding Chinese lunged at John Chang, thrusting the tip of his *chiang* lance at the detective's throat. Chang dodged the spear and quickly grabbed the shaft behind the blade. His leg shot out in a high sidekick. The Tong aggressor's head snapped back forcibly when Chang's foot crashed into his face. The detective easily wrenched the spear from the dazed man's grasp and cracked the red oak shaft against the side of his opponent's skull. Another Tong fell, never to offer any threat to anyone again. Chang made certain of that by plunging the *chiang* into the man's heart.

Two Tong enforcers attacked Clint Adams. One swung a sword overhead while the other brandished a *fu* hatchet in each fist. The Gunsmith's pistol roared. The swordsman dropped his weapon and staggered backward. His hands clawed at the bullet hole in his throat. Blood oozed between his fingers as he crumpled to the floor.

Clint whirled and triggered the Colt again. A forty-five slug smashed into the left ribcage of the hatchet-wielding Tong. The man spun about from the impact of the bullet. The Gunsmith stepped forward and shoved a boot into the wounded man's rump, sending him stumbling into two other Tong killers.

Sam Wing also decided the time to start shooting had arrived. He fired his Smith & Wesson at a Tong warrior armed with a pair of fighting knives. The man tumbled to the floor with a forty-four round in his chest.

Another Chinese killer swung a *chang-kan* stave. The rock maple fighting stick struck Wing's forearm, jarring the S&W from the deective's hand. The Tong assailant followed up with a thrust for Wing's solar plexus, using the end of his stave like a bayonet.

Wing sidestepped the attack and seized his opponent's weapon. The detective pulled hard, increasing the Tong aggressor's own forward momentum. Wing suddenly fell back, landing on his rump and rolling on his back as he raised a foot to meet the Tong's midriff. Sam pumped his leg hard and kicked the killer into an unexpected somersault. The man hurled over Wing's head and crashed to the floor hard.

Clint saw a Yellow Serpent piece of filth confront Chang, whirling a three-section staff at the detective. Chang ducked under the flexible weapon and dove to the floor, executing a fast shoulder roll to put more distance between himself and his opponent. He completed the move and landed on one knee, his short-barreled Colt drawn from its shoulder holster.

The man with the three-section staff stared at Chang, startled to find himself facing a man with a gun. The detective opened fire. A forty-four slug hit the Tong enforcer in the stomach. He doubled up and John triggered his weapon once more, drilling a bullet through the dome of the man's bowed head.

The Tong goon Clint had shot in a lung feebly tried to rise from the floor. The Gunsmith hammered the butt of his revolver into the nape of the man's neck. The Chinese slumped unconscious, unaware his life was bleeding onto the floor.

Wing finished off the last opponent by seizing the

dazed man from behind and twisting his head with all his might. Bone crunched. The detective released his opponent. The man fell on his belly, but his lifeless face stared up at the ceiling.

"Everybody okay?" Clint asked, watching the doorway which led to the next room.

"Do Tong bastards count?" Wing asked as he retrieved his S&W pistol.

"Hell, no," the Gunsmith replied.

"Then everybody is okay," the detective announced.

The trio headed for the parlor. The Gunsmith noticed that the French furniture had been rearranged to form a barrier blocking entrance to the hallway. He suspected the blockade might serve another purpose as well.

"Get back!" he shouted.

The detectives leaped to the cover of one doorway while Clint Adams dove to the other. They moved just in time. A shotgun bellowed from the barrier. Buckshot sprayed the area where the three men had formerly been a second before the Gunsmith voiced his warning. The report of a pistol was almost lost amid the roar of the scattergun.

"Draw their fire," Clint told his friends. "But be careful."

The detectives pointed their pistols at the barrier and fired two rounds each at the furniture. Chang and Wing immediately retreated behind the doorway. Exposing only one eye, Clint watched the twin muzzles of a Greener shotgun appear between a sofa and a chair. The scattergun belched another load of buckshot, blasting pellets into the doorway where Chang and Wing were stationed.

Then a Chinese gunman rose up with a pistol and aimed it at the detectives' position. Clint immediately raised his modified Colt and squeezed the trigger. A 240-grain projectile burst through the side of the Tong enforcer's head. His skull exploded, plastering blood and brains on the nearest wall.

When enemy fire did not immediately respond, the Gunsmith took the chance that the shotgunner on the other side of the barrier was now alone. He fired a fast double-action round at the Tong's position and dashed forward. Clint threw himself to the floor and slid to the edge of the furniture bunker.

A lone Chinese was huddled behind the barrier. He held the Greener in one hand with the gun broken open, about to insert a fresh shell into one of the barrels. The man saw Clint and desperately snapped his shotgun shut to attempt to use it. The Gunsmith aimed his forty-five and shot the Chinese in the face, drilling a bullet through the bridge of his nose, into his brain.

"Okay," the Gunsmith called out. "It's clear."

The detectives advanced quickly and joined Clint. The Gunsmith gathered up the Greener and broke it open. There was one shell in the breech. He located the cartridge the Tong goon had been about to load into the weapon before Clint arrived. The Gunsmith inserted it into the other barrel and closed the scattergun.

"The hall seems to be deserted," John Chang remarked, cautiously peering into the next room.

"There isn't much cover in there unless a fella tries to hide behind a potted plant," the Gunsmith explained. "Our main problem will be trying to get up those stairs before the Tong can cut us down."

"How many men do you think they have left?" Sam Wing inquired as he found the pistol which had formerly belonged to the other Chinese hoodlum. "We've taken out more than a dozen already."

"It only takes one to kill you," the Gunsmith remarked as he began to reload his Colt revolver.

Chapter Thirty

The Gunsmith led the way to the stairwell. He held the twelve-gauge Greener in his fists. The modified Colt was thrust into his belt. Sam Wing followed, his S&W in one fist and the Remington forty-four he'd taken from the dead Tong in the other. John Chang, armed only with his short-barreled Colt, brought up the rear.

Clint Adams gazed up the stairs, watching for any sign of the ambush he was certain was waiting for them. Holding the shotgun ready, the Gunsmith began to ascend the stairs.

Suddenly, three Chinese killers appeared at the head of the stairs. Two aimed shotguns at Clint and the detectives. The third Tong member awkwardly pointed a pistol at the trio. Unfortunately for the Tong enforcers, the Yellow Serpent Society had never bothered to train their followers in the use of firearms.

Mao Chu had left the instruction of his men's combat skills in the hands of Ming Chuan and other *wu-shu* experts who taught traditional Chinese martial arts. Although the Chinese had invented gunpowder centuries ago, firearms were invented in Europe. The *wu-shu* traditionalists tended to dismiss guns, thinking that all one needed to do was point the weapon, cock it

169

and pull the trigger. Why would anyone need to practice such a simple process?

Clint and the two detectives, however, were American born and raised. The United States had always had a tradition of the gun. Unlike the Tong, the Gunsmith and his allies did not have to fumble with unfamiliar weapons.

The Gunsmith's Greener bellowed, spitting fire and buckshot before the Oriental hoodlums could operate weapons they'd never handled until that very night. Two Tong enforcers were struck in the face and chest by lead pellets which shredded flesh and shattered bone. Their corpses were hurtled back into the nearest wall and slid to the floor, twin globs of pulverized meat.

The third Tong gunman had received three stray buckshot pellets as well. The man's left arm was torn and bloodied by the tiny projectiles. He almost dropped his shotgun as he staggered for shelter. Sam Wing's Smith & Wesson snarled, drilling a forty-four round into the wounded man's back. The bullet struck him under the left shoulder blade and tunneled into his heart.

Clint boldly dashed up the stairs, followed by the two detectives. He reached the head of the stairs, swinging the shotgun from side to side, searching for the enemy. A Tong enforcer poked his head out of a room and hastily retreated. The Gunsmith held his fire.

Wing and Chang joined Clint in the second story hallway. They glanced at the rows of doors, guns held ready and cocked in their fists. The Gunsmith jerked his head toward one end of the corridor.

"You two watch that side," he instructed. "Cover my back."

"We check the rooms one by one?" Wing asked.

"No other way to be sure we get them all," Clint replied.

"*Gung-djee!*" a voice shouted as a door popped open.

"Attack," Chang translated for Clint's sake.

Several other doors suddenly burst open. Tong enforcers poured out into the hallway. Some held guns, others prepared to hurl *fu* hatchets and throw knives at Clint and the detectives.

The Gunsmith pulled the other shotgun trigger. The second shotgun barrel released its murderous load. Buckshot smashed into the closely grouped Chinese thugs. Mangled bodies tumbled into the Tong members fortunate enough to avoid the deadly hail of lead pellets.

Flame jetted from both pistols in Sam Wing's fists. Two Chinese recoiled from forty-four-caliber slugs slamming into their chests. Wing dropped to one knee and thumbed back the hammers of his revolvers while John Chang took careful aim with his Colt.

The diminutive detective wasn't fast with a gun, but he was accurate. Chang squeezed the trigger and put a bullet into the forehead of a Tong zealot. A split second later, Wing's pistols snarled again. One Tong caught a slug in the stomach while another man's sternum was shattered by a forty-four-lead messenger.

The latter man collapsed with bone shrapnel in his heart and lungs. The Chinese with the belly wound, however, managed to fire his thirty-two-caliber S&W pocket pistol. Sam Chang cursed and spun about sharply, the Remington revolver falling from his left hand.

"Sam!" Chang shouted in alarm when he realized

his partner had been shot.

The little detective quickly trained his Colt on the wounded Tong gunman and pumped a forty-four into the goon's face. The hoodlum's left cheekbone exploded and an eyeball popped from its cracked socket. Chang fired his pistol again and put another bullet through the man's upper jaw. Teeth spilled from the Tong enforcer's mouth. The man indeed lost face for the last time before he died.

Clint Adams's battle with the Tong followers was far from over. After sending two more Chinese hoodlums to their ancestors and wounding two other men with the shotgun blast, three of the Tong ambushers were still unharmed. The Gunsmith held the shotgun in his left fist and reached for his modified Colt revolver with his right.

Two of the remaining Tong actually had pistols in their fists, but they hesitated long enough for Clint to draw his six-gun. Once again, the Yellow Serpent Society's failure to teach their people to properly handle a firearm in combat allowed the Gunsmith to turn the tables on his opponents.

Clint's forty-five barked twice, the reports of the gunshots tumbling together to create a single deep-throated roar. Two Tong gunmen were thrown to the end of the corridor. They slammed into a wall and leaned into each other as they slid to the floor. The pair would have been comical if their faces hadn't been smashed by bullets.

The third uninjured member of the Chinese ambush team recovered from his astonishment at seeing his comrades cut down in less than a minute. He screamed in maniacal rage and lunged forward, with a hatchet in one fist and a knife in the other.

Clint pointed his pistol at the advancing figure and squeezed the trigger, but one of the wounded Chinese suddenly reached up from the floor and grabbed the Gunsmith's sleeve. The unexpected tug pulled Clint's arm down, altering the aim of his pistol when he fired the gun. A forty-five slug tore into the blade-wielding Chinese's left thigh instead of his chest.

The Tong attacker howled in pain when his femur bone splintered from the impact of the bullet. He stumbled and fell to all fours. Clint quickly clubbed the heavy iron barrels of the Greener into the skull of the man who'd grabbed his sleeve. The hand fell away from Clint's arm as gray slime dribbled from its owner's cranium.

The man with the shattered leg snarled and hurled his *fu* hatchet at the Gunsmith. Clint barely weaved his head in time to avoid the deadly projectile. The hatchet slammed into the wall near his head. The sharp blade bit into the plaster surface hard.

"Your turn," Clint hissed. "Try to dodge this."

He shot the man between the eyes.

"Clint!" Chang's voice cried.

The Gunsmith turned to see the detective kneeling beside Sam Wing. Chang's partner sat on the floor with his back against a wall. Wing's jacket had been stripped off and Chang was gingerly removing the leather strap of Wing's shoulder holster from his left arm.

"How bad was Sam hit?" Clint asked as he rushed forward to help his friends.

"I just caught one in the shoulder," Wing answered. "Feels like my collarbone might be broken. . . ."

"I think the bullet is lodged in the bone," Chang stated. "It's got to come out, Clint."

"How's the bleeding?" the Gunsmith inquired.

"Oh, it's bleeding just fine." Wing chuckled. "Hurts like hell too."

"Good," Clint commented. "That means you probably don't have any nerve damage and the artery wasn't severed. No internal bleeding."

"Uh-huh," Wing replied through clenched teeth. "Ain't I lucky?"

"Shut up and rest," Chang snapped.

"I'll rest," Wing stated. "You two find Amanda."

"We can't just leave you—" Chang began.

"You're not going to perform five-minute surgery either," Wing snapped. "Go on. I'll still be here when you get back."

"Let's check these rooms, John," Clint suggested. "The sooner we find Amanda, the sooner we can get Sam to a doctor."

Chang nodded in agreement.

The Gunsmith and John Chang moved from room to room and kicked in the doors. With weapons held ready, they checked inside each compartment. Every room was empty. No sign of Amanda.

Then they approached the last door, Clint moved to the right of the door. Chang moved to the left. The detective slammed a heel kick into the door and it swung open. Two pistols snarled from the room within. Bullets sizzled through air between the Gunsmith and Chang who continued to use the door frame for cover.

Clint cautiously peered into the room and spied two nervous Tong enforcers standing beside a bed. He immediately swung his pistol through the doorway and squeezed the trigger. A Tong killer's head hopped violently from the impact of a forty-five bullet that crashed into it.

The Gunsmith aimed his weapon at the other goon and squeezed the trigger again. The hammer clicked on an empty chamber.

The Chinese hootowl fired two rounds at the Gunsmith. Bullets chewed splinters from the door-frame as Clint retreated behind it. Chang's Colt exploded in response. Clint heard a man scream inside the room and saw Chang rush in after his opponent.

The Gunsmith followed. The Tong hoodlum had been wounded by the detective's bullet. His right arm hung uselessly as he stared in horror at the furious John Chang who attacked him. The detective whipped the heel of his left hand under the thug's chin. The man's head snapped back from the blow. Chang's right hand immediately slashed an edge of the palm stroke to his adversary's throat.

As the Tong enforcer collapsed into a corner, choking to death on a crushed windpipe, Clint approached the bed. Amanda Lincoln lay on the mattress. Her naked body was marred by bruises and scratches, but she raised her head and smiled at the two rescuers.

"Thank God you found me!" she cried with relief.

"Amanda." Chang moved to the bed. "Did they hurt you? That's a stupid question. . . ."

"Just get me out of here, please," Amanda replied.

The Gunsmith checked the pistols of the slain Tong members. One gun was an old Navy Colt cap and ball revolver. Clint discarded it and checked the other weapon. He nodded with satisfaction as he examined the forty-five-caliber British Tranter.

"You'd better reload your gun," Clint advised as he removed the shells from the Tranter. Only two cartridges hadn't been fired.

"It sounds pretty quiet out there," Chang replied.

"Mao Chu and Ming Chuan are still around here somewhere," Clint said, loading the forty-five shells into his Colt.

They wrapped Amanda in a sheet and helped her into the corridor. The hallway was littered with corpses, many the grisly victims of buckshot blasts and multiple bullet wounds. Chang noticed Sam Wing's body was slumped limply against the wall.

"No!" he exclaimed, dashing to his partner's inert form.

Clint and Amanda joined Chang. The Gunsmith sighed with relief when he saw Wing's diaphragm rise and fall. Chang checked his partner's pulse and peeled back an eyelid.

"He passed out," the detective announced. "We'll have to carry him."

"Okay," Clint began. "See if—"

A fierce battle cry drew their attention to the stairs. A lone Tong soldier charged up the stairs with a *chiang* spear in his fists. The Gunsmith whirled and fired his Colt. A forty-five in the chest sent the man tumbling down the stairs.

"I'll go first," Clint said. "You look after Amanda and Sam until I tell you to come ahead."

"You just want to avoid having to carry him." Chang grinned.

"Stay alert, John," the Gunsmith warned. "We're not out of this mess yet, but we're pretty close now. No time to get careless."

"Agreed." Chang nodded. "Just remember your own advice, my friend."

Clint descended the stairs slowly. He realized he only had one shell left in his pistol. Halfway to the foot of the stairs, he considered going back for another gun.

The hall below seemed deserted, but he decided it would be a needless risk to check the place without ample firepower. Clint started to back up the stairs.

Without warning, a hand appeared over the rail. Powerful fingers clamped around the Gunsmith's wrist. His finger involuntarily tightened on the trigger. The Colt roared, blasting a useless round into the ceiling.

A hard pull sent Clint stumbling down the remaining steps. He managed to keep his balance until his foot slipped on the second to last riser. The Gunsmith fell to the floor, his empty pistol skidding beyond reach.

"Wang-pu-tan!" a harsh voice snarled.

Clint looked up to see a sinister figure emerge from the side of the staircase. Ming Chuan smiled as he approached the Gunsmith. Clint scrambled to his feet. The *chuan-shu* killer raised his deadly hands—hands that could kill with a single blow.

"Oh, shit," the Gunsmith muttered hopelessly.

Chapter Thirty-One

Clint Adams balled his fists in a defensive stance. Ming Chuan's hands were poised like a pair of cobras. The fingers were held in a clawlike manner. The Gunsmith could only guess what kind of attack the deadly martial artist was about to launch.

So he decided to strike first.

The Gunsmith advanced quickly and feinted a left jab. He then threw a desperate kick at his opponent's groin. Ming Chuan drove a ram's head punch into Clint's shin. It felt as if the Chinese had hit him with a hickory cudgel.

Clint swung a right cross at his opponent's grinning face. Ming Chuan easily ducked under Clint's whirling fist and slammed the front of his elbow into the Gunsmith's stomach. Clint doubled up with a gasp, his breath spewing from his lungs like air from a leaky balloon.

The big Chinese moved behind Clint and delivered a hand chop to the small of the Gunsmith's back. Clint cried out, certain his spine had been broken by the vicious blow. Ming Chuan's steel talon fingers grabbed the back of Clint's neck, thumb and fingers squeezing the carotid arteries. The Gunsmith rammed an elbow into his opponent. It struck a wall of hard muscle. Ming Chuan didn't even grunt.

The Gunsmith tried to gulp air into his aching lungs as he felt himself drifting into a black void. It was as if he were drowning, but nothing was pouring into his lungs. They were empty. Clint made a feeble effort to pry the fingers from his neck, but he didn't have enough strength left to even get a firm grip on Ming Chuan's pinkie.

Suddenly, the Chinese simply tossed Clint across the room. The Gunsmith crashed into a wall and fell beside his discarded Colt revolver. For a split second he lay dazed, relishing the sweet joy of air flowing into his tortured lungs. His head cleared rapidly and he grabbed the Colt, finding security in the feel of the familiar weapon.

Then he gazed up to see Ming Chuan. The Oriental gestured at Clint to get up.

It's a game for him, the Gunsmith thought. *The son of a bitch could have killed me. He wants to make me sweat before he finishes me off.*

Clint rose from the floor with the empty revolver in his fist. He held the gun by its barrel, ready to use the walnut butt for a club. Ming Chuan shook his head and laughed at the Gunsmith's attempt to defend himself.

''Let's see if you think this is funny,'' Clint snarled as he raised the pistol overhead.

Ming Chuan prepared to block or dodge the attack. Clint used the distraction to strike from a different direction. His left fist shot out and hit the Tong killer squarely on the bridge of the nose. Ming Chuan's head recoiled and blood trickled from a nostril.

He's human after all, the Gunsmith thought as he swung the revolver at his adversary's skull.

The Chinese caught Clint's wrist before the gun butt could strike its target. Ming Chuan's other hand grabbed the Gunsmith's belt and he suddenly lifted Clint off his feet and hurled him to the floor like a bag of rice.

The Gunsmith landed hard. He lay on his back, stunned and once again bordering on unconsciousness. Through a gray mist, he saw Ming Chuan charge forward and raise a foot high. Clint rolled to the right and his opponent's shoe stomped the floor where his head had formerly been.

Clint quickly hammered the butt of his Colt into the man's instep. Ming Chuan roared in pain and hopped away from the Gunsmith. Clint scrambled to his feet only to receive a powerful sidekick to the chest which propelled him across the room.

The Gunsmith tripped over the corpse of the Tong goon he'd previously shot on the stairs. Clint fell once more and again lost his grip on the revolver. Ming Chuan rushed forward and kicked the gun beyond Clint's reach.

Clint rolled away from his opponent. His hand brushed against a hard object. In desperation, Clint grabbed it before he realized he'd found the dead man's *chiang* spear. He slashed the lance at Ming Chuan who retreated in surprise.

The Gunsmith rose from the floor, holding the unfamiliar weapon in his fists. Clint had never handled a spear before. The confident smile on Ming Chuan's face revealed that the Chinese realized this as well. The Gunsmith didn't bother trying to imitate any fancy *wu-shu* techniques. He simply lunged at Ming Chuan.

The big Chinese quickly sidestepped away from the thrusting blade of the lance. He lashed a hand at the shaft between Clint's fists. Wood snapped as the spear broke in two.

Ming Chuan followed up with a backfist to Clint's jaw. The Gunsmith staggered, blood oozing from his mouth. His feet seemed to slip as his legs lost their strength. Clint fell to one knee, a broken half of the *chiang* spear still clenched in each fist.

The big Chinese flexed his fingers and smiled. Clint gazed up at Ming Chuan's mocking smile. The Tong killer gestured for Clint to try one more time. The murderous glint in his onyx black eyes warned the Gunsmith that his formidable adversary had grown weary of the game and decided to let Clint try one last charge before killing him.

Clint began to rise. His breath was ragged and uneven. Every muscle in his body seemed to be bruised, knotted or pulled out of place. The Gunsmith had to succeed with his next move. He didn't have enough strength left to continue fighting. If he failed, Ming Chuan would break his neck as easily as he had the shaft of the lance.

The Gunsmith's arm flashed as he hurled a piece of the broken spear at Ming Chuan. The *wu-shu* expert easily weaved his head to avoid the missile. At the same instant, Clint dove forward, both fists clenched around the other spear half, the metal point aimed at his opponent's solar plexus.

Ming Chuan didn't move fast enough this time. The sharp spear blade bit into flesh. Clint shoved hard, driving the lance upward. The blade punched through muscle and pierced Ming Chuan's heart.

The Chinese brute bellowed in agony. He slashed the side of his hand at Clint's head, trying to take the Gunsmith with him to the grave. Clint ducked under the deadly swipe and threw himself to the floor, rolling away from the wounded assassin.

Ming Chuan fell to his knees. Blood soaked his

cotton jacket as he seized the splintered shaft that jutted from his chest. The Tong enforcer pulled forcibly and ripped the spear from his chest. This only served to uncork an even greater flow of blood from his pierced heart. Ming Chuan slumped to the floor—dead.

"Congratulations, Mr. Adams," a voice announced calmly. "You've won."

Clint recognized the voice of Mao Chu. The Tong leader spoke from the parlor beyond the hallway. Gathering himself up from the floor, the battered Gunsmith staggered to the doorway and peered into the next room.

Mao Chu sat in an armchair, his feet braced on the corpse of one of his slain followers. The head of the Yellow Serpent Society held a long-stemmed pipe to his lips. He drew on it, drawing smoke deep into his lungs. The smell of opium filled the room.

"What sort of trick do you have up your sleeve this time, Mao?" Clint demanded as he leaned against the doorway, breathing hard from the incredible exhaustion that followed his battle with Ming Chuan.

"I have no tricks left, Mr. Adams," the Tong boss assured him. "I've lost. Allow me to accept defeat with grace."

"Hell," the Gunsmith muttered, "I think I know you well enough to figure you're not going to sit there and smoke that crap until you drift into a stupor while we leave here to get the police."

"The opium kills the pain, Mr. Adams," Mao replied.

"The pain of defeat?" Clint sneered.

"Of cyanide poison," Mao explained. "I swallowed a capsule when I saw you kill Ming Chuan.

Cyanide is quick, but it isn't without pain. I've seen men die from poison before. My life has been filled with pain. I'd like to have my death contain as little as possible.''

Mao's body began to tremble. He bit on the stem of the pipe and sucked desperately. His eyes squinted in pain as he clawed at the constriction in his chest.

"Do . . . you . . . understand, Mr. Ad—'' Mao's sentence ended abruptly as his body stiffened. The opium pipe slipped from his mouth and his fingers dug into his chest.

"I don't know if you can hear me, Mao," the Gunsmith stated. "But I think I understand. The Yellow Serpent Society was your life. It was your business, your family, your private empire. You have nothing left but the life in your body which is no longer of any value to you.''

Mao managed a tense smile and nodded in response. Then he slumped in the chair and died.

Chapter Thirty-Two

Inspector Kovac and Clint Adams emerged from the police station and descended the stairs. The policeman offered a cigar to the Gunsmith. Clint shook his head.

"Wish you'd take it," Kovac said. "Sort of like accepting my apology."

"Apology accepted," the Gunsmith assured him. "Just make sure the newspapers print a complete story about my innocence. I don't want to go through life with folks wondering if I murdered a woman."

"Don't worry about that," Kovac promised. "The story will be on the front page tomorrow morning."

"Keep it on the front page for a couple days," Clint told him. "Tell about Mao Chu and what happened tonight in tomorrow's paper. Then the next story can be about Shin Chi's confession and details he'll give you. Then you can tell the papers about your final investigation of Mao Chu's estate and whatever you turn up at the Flowers of Paradise."

"I can't promise that the newspapers will go along with that," Kovac said helplessly.

"Sure you can," the Gunsmith replied. "Just tell them part of the story each time you talk to them. The police commissioner and the mayor will agree to it. If they don't, I'll just have to sue the San Francisco Police Department for false arrest, defamation of character, slander, libel—whatever I can manage."

"That's blackmail." Kovac frowned.

"I don't care what you call it, but I've got a bank account with a bundle of cash saved up. I can buy a couple of good lawyers who play dirty and I'll take this to court and get everything I can out of it unless your people agree to my terms."

"Shit," Kovac muttered. "We'll see what we can do, Adams."

"Kind of thought you'd see it my way." The Gunsmith grinned.

"Yeah," Kovac said sourly. "How's Sam Wing doing?"

"The bullet just winged Sam," Clint replied, "if you'll pardon my play on words. The doctor said his left arm will be in a sling for a while, but the collarbone ought to knit back into place and he'll be good as new in a couple of months."

"He and John Chang will sure get a lot of publicity," Kovac remarked. "They'll probably wind up with more business than they can handle."

"They deserve it," Clint said. "Besides, the publicity should be welcomed by the police. The destruction of the Yellow Serpent Society will be a warning to the other Tongs that they'd better not go too far."

"Christ, I hope so." The inspector sighed. "I don't want to have to go through another mess like this."

"Me either," the Gunsmith agreed. "Well, if you don't have more questions for me, I'd like to head to the livery and check on Duke and my wagon."

"Planning to leave San Francisco soon?" Kovac asked, his tone suggesting he'd welcome an affirmative answer.

"Hell no," Clint replied. "I came here to sell my services as a gunsmith, remember? Reckon it's about time I quit fooling around and got back to work."